# BURIED
## IN
# TREASURE

Books in the Mackenzie Prentice Mysteries Series

October Fire
Buried in Treasure
Painted Lady
On the Edge
Old Habits
My Cousin Krissy (2026)

# BURIED IN TREASURE

## A MACKENZIE PRENTICE MYSTERY

# MARY PIERCE

Seven Windows LLC

For loving caregivers everywhere,
for those who trust them,
and for my mother, who trusted me.

There was a crooked man, who walked a crooked mile.
He found a crooked sixpence upon a crooked stile.
He bought a crooked cat, which caught a crooked mouse,
And they all lived together in a little crooked house.

—Mother Goose

For where your treasure is, there your heart will be also.

Luke 12:34

# CHAPTER ONE

M Y GRANDMOTHER TELLS ME, "Mackenzie, you're either in a problem, just came out of one, or heading toward one. That's life."

I tell Gram, "That sucks."

Gram tells me, "Watch your mouth."

I watch my mouth. When Gram says do, you do. Even if you're thirty-five.

But Gram's right about life, of course, and I was deluded in thinking that I'd had all the problems I was going to have lately. I'd buried my ex-husband, lost my job, gotten dumped, lost my apartment to a fire, was almost shot, and then almost burned up. All within a couple of weeks. *Whew*.

I thought maybe I'd get a break from trouble, at least for a little while. But life had other plans for me.

If you'd told me those plans would include my trying to figure out how an old man died, driving around in a car full of crickets, and ending up in a boys' locker room with my face in a urinal, I would not have believed you.

But I need to start at the beginning.

SUNDAY MORNING. NOVEMBER 11. VETERANS DAY.

Gram and her third husband, Nathan, had just returned from Our Savior's Lutheran, one of a dozen Lutheran churches in Three Rivers. That's a lot of Lutherans for a town of 20,000 people.

Gram had asked earlier that morning if I'd like to come to church with them.

"Too tired," I mumbled, sinking deeper under the pink covers of the incredibly soft bed in the Rose Room of Gram's Victorian house where I'm staying. Temporarily, I tell myself. Very temporarily.

Gram laid her cool hand on my forehead, brushed my cheek oh-so-gently. "Of course, Mackenzie, dear. You need your rest after all you've been through. Maybe next week." She was so sweet I felt guilty, but not guilty enough to get up.

When I heard Gram and Nathan return from church, I forced my body out of that downy-soft comfort. I put on a pair of gray sweatpants and a Three Rivers marathon tee shirt, both borrowed from my mother, the runner. My clothes were still at my burned-out apartment, waiting for the okay for me to go back and retrieve them. Assuming there was anything left to retrieve.

I layered on a white sweatshirt of Gram's with a pair of cardinals cozied up together on a pine branch. *Lucky birds,* Lonely Me whispered.

I had no one in my life, romantically speaking, since my last relationship—if I could even call it that—ended abruptly. Then there was a guy named Frank who said he'd call but hadn't. Ditto for a cop named Ben. *Where are the guys who keep their word? Where are the men who stay?*

I don't get it. I have a nice smile and cool green eyes. My brown hair varies in style and color—a disaster at times, but that makes me more interesting, right? I'm not gorgeous, but I've been called cute. Average. Not too tall, not too short, not too fat, not too thin. I'm pretty smart, and I can be funny. And, according to my late ex-husband, not a bad kisser.

*So, what's the problem?* Lonely Me asked. I had no answers.

The smell of frying bacon drew me downstairs. I swung through the front parlor and said good morning to my para-keets, Chirp and Tweet, whom I'd saved from the apartment fire. I chirped at Tweet, and Chirp tweeted back. Or maybe it was the other way around. Hard to be sure.

I went into Gram's cheery green and yellow kitchen. My mother, Barbara, stood at the stove making french toast. She had Gram's Kiss the Cook apron over her church clothes and her long brown hair pulled into a ponytail. Gram and Nathan sat at the table, drinking coffee and holding hands.

As I walked in, my mother ordered, "Get the syrup pitcher out of the microwave."

"Are you talking to me, Mom?" *Good morning to you too.* Snarky Me was awake.

"Yes, you! And the pitcher is hot. Be careful!"

"Gee, thanks for the warning, Mommy," I said, Snarky adding more than a skosh of sarcasm. Did my mother really think I didn't have any common sense? Maybe that was it, or maybe it was just that my mother has always been anxious. About everything. All the time.

As I set the syrup on the table, she snapped at me again. "Have you washed your hands?"

"Yes, Mommy! Look!" I walked over and wiggled my fingers in her face. She jabbed her elbow at me. I dodged it.

"Don't be so snotty. Now go! Sit!"

*Yes, Mommy. Right away, Mommy! Geez!* How old does a girl have to be before she stops being annoyed by her mother? Older than I am, obviously.

It's annoying to be thirty-five years old and living with my mommy. Actually, my mother and I are both living here in Gram's house. I'm here because the apartment fire left me homeless.

My mother, Barbara, is sixty-two and has been divorced since I was a kid. She moved in a year ago to help my eighty-year-old grandmother care for Nathan. He's eighty-two, and is, as he puts it, "losing his marbles."

My mother may be anxious and, at times, controlling, but I give her credit. She raised us five kids (I'm the lucky middle child) to healthy, relatively stable adulthood, and she did it on her own after my father left to get cigarettes one night and never came back. She moved us from The City to Three Rivers to be closer to family just as I started middle school.

I gave Nathan and Gram each a little hug around the shoulders before I sat down.

Gram turned to me. "The ceremony is at one o'clock. You're coming, aren't you, Mackenzie?"

"Wouldn't miss it," I said.

The Three Rivers town council hosts a Veterans Day ceremony honoring all who wear or have ever worn a uniform. A community "thank you for your service."

Nathan is a veteran of the Korean War, and he and Gram

are super patriotic. The American flag flies on Gram's porch year-round. I have asked her about the rules that say you should take the flag down in bad weather and at night.

"Just need to light it after dark," Gram once said. And whatever it's made of, that flag has withstood years of rain, snow, sleet, and hail. She said, "This flag is guaranteed not to fade, mildew, or rot."

"So, it's plastic," I said.

"Don't make jokes. It's the flag we're talking about," she'd said, a note of reverence in her voice.

This morning, Nathan sat at the table finishing his french toast. Tall and slim with thick white hair, Nathan was in great physical shape in his seventies when he and Gram met a decade ago. They met on a cruise, ballroom dancing.

Lately, Nathan's memory has been coming and going, so we all live in what Gram calls "the reality of the moment."

Gram brushed lint off his army jacket, retrieved from the attic and hanging on the back of a chair. Dust motes floated in the sunlight coming through the window above the sink. I fake-coughed, waving my hand. "Geez, Louise. That's one dusty ol' uniform," I said.

Nathan looked at me. "Whose uniform is it?"

"Yours, Nathan."

He winked and smiled. "Just kidding, Mackenzie."

*Ah,* I thought, *Nathan is all present and accounted for at the moment.* I thought that until he turned to Gram and said, "I need to call Clark. Make sure he's not late for the ceremony."

Gram frowned. "Clark? I'm sorry, Nathan, but Clark's not going to be able to be here today."

Nathan's face fell. "That's a shame. Clark loves this kind of stuff."

Gram shot me a look. We'd been through this before. Gram didn't have the heart to tell him—again—that his brother, Clark, had passed away last year. With memory loss, you tell the person they've lost their brother, and then you have to tell them again. And again. Gram had said, "It's cruel to keep giving someone such painful news over and over." I agreed.

So, whenever Nathan mentions Clark, Gram tells a "fiblet." Clark is away on a trip. Maybe he can come next week. With a fiblet, you stay vague. Change the subject.

When Gram first did this, my mother was incensed. "How can you lie to him like that?"

Gram explained. "Because this is kinder. I don't want him to feel worse by reminding him he's forgotten something or gotten confused." My mother and I had both come around to Gram's way of thinking. It did feel kinder.

Nathan seemed to accept Gram's fiblet as she held the jacket toward him. "Let's see how it fits."

Nathan stood, then pulled the belt tighter at the waist of his baggy wool uniform pants. "Don't want these to fall off!" he said with a grin. Gram held the jacket as Nathan slipped into it. The jacket hung loose.

"Lookin' good, Nathan," I said. I thought of the cartoon of the middle-aged man trying on his old army uniform, claiming it still fits, even as the buttons are popping off because he's gained weight. In Nathan's case, the opposite was true. Never an overweight guy, he'd lost even more weight lately.

Nathan adjusted the garrison cap over his white hair. "At least the hat still fits. My head hasn't shrunk!"

As Gram buttoned his jacket, Nathan said, "Can't wait to see Clark there today!"

Gram gave a sigh. "No, dear, Clark isn't coming."

Nathan furrowed his brow. "Did I say Clark? Sorry. I meant Cliff."

Gram and Nathan had been good friends with Cliff and Florence Wilson. After Florence died of cancer three years ago, Gram had said, "I've seen plenty of grief, but Florence's death seems to have taken all the light from Cliff's life. I worry that he's never going to come out of it."

Cliff's health started to decline. His late wife's niece and nephew moved in to help him out. Jillian and Jason were twins, both single and in their early forties. Other than the twins and Florence's cousin Sadie in New Jersey, Cliff had no remaining family.

Cliff started to have episodes of dizziness and falling and some hallucinations. "He imagined he saw Florence in the house," Gram told me. "Maybe he's getting dementia."

Despite his health, Cliff continued playing cribbage with Nathan at the Three Rivers senior center on Wednesday mornings with another vet named Jack. The three had served in Korea at the same time, though they hadn't known each other back then.

Gram smiled as she adjusted the shoulders on Nathan's army jacket. "You look so handsome," she said as she smoothed the jacket's shoulders with her palms.

Nathan saluted her. "Thank you, ma'am."

She planted a kiss on his cheek. "You're welcome, sweetheart. And I'm sure Cliff will be there today."

But Gram was wrong about that. Cliff wouldn't be going anywhere anytime soon.

# CLIFF

The house itself—a Craftsman-style bungalow built in the late 1930s—probably wasn't going to be worth much. He and Florence bought the house in 1952 after he got back from Korea. Cliff had never been keen on home improvement projects and had neglected even routine home maintenance for the past decade. That's when Florence was diagnosed with lung cancer.

It took five years for her to die. She was on hospice that last year, fighting. Cliff told his buddy Nathan that he felt like he was watching someone drown, except they were drowning in their own lungs.

When Cliff closed his eyes, he could still see her there in their double bed, battling for breath as he cradled her in his arms. Then, at last, that one final gasp, and she lay still. Time stopped for her. For them both.

Eventually, he felt the spell break, laid her gently against the pillow, called the hospice nurse, and let Florence go.

Family and friends paid their respects at the funeral. Florence's niece Jillian and her twin brother, Jason—the closest local family. Florence's cousin Sadie came all the way from New Jersey. That was nice of her. Of course, their good friends Nathan and Virginia were there, along with Virginia's daughter Barbara and her children. Cliff especially liked Virginia's granddaughter Mackenzie. Other friends—Jack from the senior center and their neighbors, the Crandalls next door, and others— brought casseroles that would sit in the kitchen uneaten. Cliff had no appetite. Why eat when you've lost your reason to live?

One day, a few months after the funeral, when people had stopped calling and stopped dropping by, Cliff went for a walk. One of the neighbors was having a garage sale, and Cliff wandered in. A stack of eight record albums with a handwritten tag: Vintage Vinyl $5.00.

He flipped through the albums, memories of Florence washing over him. The two of them melting together as they danced to "The Last Waltz." Florence singing along with Patsy Cline. "Crazy." "I Fall to Pieces." "Walking after Midnight." Florence knew them all.

"Five bucks each?" he asked the guy sitting in the lawn chair.

"Nope. Five for the whole stack. Old school. Gotta go," the guy said.

Cliff carried the albums—cradling them gently—back home.

Cliff's collection grew from there. Piles of albums. Then he found an old hi-fi, like discovering a dinosaur. A wooden cabinet with a radio in one side and a turntable on the other. Put a stack of LPs on the spindle, and you've got music all night long. He found another hi-fi and had to have it. Then another. Three in the living room. Nice.

Then, one day, he came upon a collection of 45s, those little records with the big center holes. He remembered when the first ones came out in 1949. "They don't make these anymore. Must be worth something," he told himself. The Crew Cuts, the Everly Brothers, Big Bopper, and Ritchie Valens. *Sh-boom sh-boom, ya-da-da da-da-da . . . Life could be a dream. Cry me a river. Chantilly lace, pretty face, ponytail hangin' down. Bye-bye, Miss American Pie.* Cliff had to have them.

Cliff could have played them on one of the big hi-fis, but he remembered a friend playing 45s on a portable record player, and he started collecting those. One, two, ten. A stack of cases piled up in the corner of the living room—beige, pink, blue, rectangular, like little suitcases with plastic handles. He smiled at the stack. They made a lovely arrangement there in the corner. Ready. Waiting.

Six months after Florence's death, Cliff found, at an estate sale, a box of blue drinking glasses. He picked one up and cried as he stood there in that dead stranger's dining room. How Florence loved the blue glasses her mother had. His mother had some too. The blue glasses came home. Then green glass. Then yellow glass. "Depression glass," people called it. For Cliff, it was grief glass.

A necklace caught his eye one day at a sale. Hadn't his mother had one just like that? He bought it and then started collecting all the costume jewelry he could find. Boxes of brooches and necklaces, rings and bracelets.

The house filled with boxes and boxes of stuff, stuff, and more stuff. Cliff was sure there was a genuine treasure in there somewhere. He'd seen it happen countless times on *Antiques Roadshow*, now one of his favorite shows.

The person would say, "What? That old thing? I was about to throw it out."

To which the appraiser would reply, "It's a good thing you didn't because it's worth—" (*drumroll, please*) and they'd name an astronomical sum.

The person would then say something like, "I promised myself I wouldn't cry," as they cried. Or "My father would be so pleased." More than once, Cliff watched and imagined being that lucky person. He'd whisper, "My wife would be so pleased." And more than once, he said out loud, "Right, Florence?" and each time, he pictured her smiling at him.

Cliff moved on from records, glass, and jewelry to birds. Florence loved birds. Anytime Cliff spotted a figurine, a piece of pottery, a plate, a cup—anything with a bird on it—he bought it. Boxes and boxes and boxes of birds.

Florence was a Wisconsin girl and a huge Green Bay Packers fan, so Cliff collected Packers stuff for her. Jerseys, cups, plates, pennants, playing cards, trading cards. Anything and everything Packers. From a garage sale, he'd scored a helmet once worn by Bart Starr, along with a life-size cardboard cutout of Brett Favre, famed Packers quarterback. Brett stood watch over the treasures from the corner of the dining room.

Sometimes, Cliff would stop and look at Brett and could almost hear the quarterback congratulating him on his collection. "It'll be worth a fortune someday," Brett would say.

At some point, Cliff started collecting magazines. Stacks of magazines fit nicely in the little spaces between stacks of boxes. What could be cooler than having fifteen years of *Sports Illustrated*? He couldn't believe his luck when some hapless sap unloaded thirty years of *National Geographic*. Another lucky score? Twenty years of *Time Magazine*. There was history there.

Speaking of history, Cliff started a small collection of things that reminded him of his time in the army during the Korean War. Pants, shirts, jackets, a couple of knives, a helmet or two, all found at garage sales or bought from fellow soldiers whose wives probably made them get rid of it. Women just didn't get how important this stuff was to a guy. Florence would have understood, of course. The war stuff wasn't likely to be worth much in the future, but Cliff didn't care about that. He kept it all as part of his own history so he wouldn't forget.

Forgetting terrified Cliff.

He'd seen it with his father, then his mother—the forgetting that came with the years. His mother looked at him, there in her last days, and frowned. "Whose kid are you?" she'd asked. The question broke his heart.

"I'm your son Cliff," he'd said.

She frowned again. "No, Cliff died in the war."

In a way, he supposed he had died for her at some point, but the war was a battle against the dementia. He'd died there on that battle-field—his mother fighting for her own mind.

So, Cliff amassed things that reminded him of his parents, his wife, the music, and the birds. He treasure-hunted every day, not noticing the piles that took over the first floor, including his bedroom, where a narrow path through boxes led to the bed he'd shared with Florence. Another path led to the only closet—Florence's closet—where every item of her clothing remained untouched, just as it was when she was alive.

Stuff filled the kitchen. Cliff ate takeout pizzas and convenience store meals, propped on his bed, watching television. The refrigerator went unused.

In the basement, wooden pantry shelves held decades-old food, home-canned by Florence, that had long since become inedible. The workbench was piled with projects—bird feeders and birdhouses mostly—he'd started before Florence passed. He'd planned to hang them outside the bedroom window so she could see the cardinals, but she died too soon.

Among the mountain of basement containers and boxes were plastic bins holding his wife's journals and letters—the history of her life, of their life together. She'd dreamed of being a writer, as did her sister, Jean. Florence's writings were entombed there, safe from the mold and mildew growing daily in that dark, dank space.

The treasure was in there, in those piles—the treasure of a man's memories. His life. Proof of his being in the world. It was the memories themselves, not the physical stuff, that were priceless, precious, the real treasure. But Cliff didn't see it that way.

The physical stuff comforted him as if Florence was still with him. Sometimes he caught the scent of her Chanel perfume. One night, he dreamed he saw her in her closet, in the silk robe she loved so much. He called her name. The light in the closet went out, and she disappeared.

Another night, he'd gone to the kitchen for a glass of water and saw her. She was at the back door in her white sweater with the red sequined cardinal on the front. He whispered her name. She walked out of the house. He ran to the door and called her name into the darkness, but she was gone.

Florence was here among the stacks. And somewhere in all of it was something that would make him rich. He was sure of it. And Florence would be pleased.

# CHAPTER TWO

THIS YEAR'S VETERANS DAY ceremony would be held, as usual, in Rawley Park. A plaque there honors "All Who Serve" with insignias for the Three Rivers police and our fire and rescue, along with the branches of the U.S. military.

At twelve-thirty, we piled into Gram's old Buick Riviera, my mother driving while I rode shotgun, and Gram and Nathan sat in back. My brother Greg and his three children met us at the park. His wife, Sarah, was home with a cold.

I sat on the metal bench of the bleachers between my two nephews, twelve-year-old Joey, and Charlie, who is ten. The boys have reddish hair and freckles like their mother. My seven-year-old niece, Violet, her blonde hair in braids, sat next to Greg. We all stood together as the Three Rivers High School band played "The Star-Spangled Banner."

That song always gets to me. Was it the serious look on my nephews' faces or the way Violet held her little hand over her little heart? Or Nathan holding a salute through the song?

Maybe it was the sense that we are all part of something bigger. Whatever. I choked back tears as we sat down.

Chief Bronson, recently retired from the Three Rivers Police Department, took the podium. I followed along in the printed program as he read a quote from the inscription on the Korean War Veterans Memorial in Washington, DC:

"Our nation honors her sons and daughters who answered the call to defend a country they never knew and a people they never met."

Incredible to think of ordinary folks, like Nathan, stepping forward, sacrificing themselves for others. I thought about all those brave people in uniform. What would it take for me to be willing to sacrifice myself? What would have to be at stake? My family? Friends? When my apartment was burning the previous month, I gave no thought to my seventy-year-old upstairs neighbor, Mrs. Litowsky. I just picked up my parakeets' cage and ran. Not my finest moment.

After the ceremony, Chief Bronson made the rounds, shaking hands with all the veterans. He shook Nathan's hand and said, "Thank you for your service." Nathan smiled, but he looked confused. Thanking people for their service is a relatively new thing.

Then the chief turned to me. We'd known each other back when my ex-husband worked for Three Rivers PD. "Hey, Mackenzie, good to see you. This your family?"

I nodded, made introductions, and then said, "Congratulations on your retirement."

"Thanks. Hey, I was sorry to hear about Billy. Damn shame about him. He was a good guy."

Snarky Me wanted to make a snarky comment about how nobody from the department had gone to my ex-husband Billy's funeral, but I decided to let it go. Billy had left the department under less-than-wonderful circumstances. I could understand there might be hard feelings.

Chief Bronson went on. "Pretty impressive how you figured out what happened to him. Gotta give you props for bringing the bad guys to justice."

I felt again the relief that it was all over, that those "bad guys" were in jail, where they belonged. "Thanks," I said. "How did you hear about that?"

"I read the paper. And you know, cops talk."

The local paper, the *Three Rivers Bulletin*, aka *The Bull*, had run an article about what happened after Billy was murdered. "How did you know it was me? They referred to me as 'Mackenzie Phillips,' like the actress."

The chief chuckled. "Not hard to figure that one out. I'm a pretty good detective too." Then he got serious. "Jesus, I heard about that whole cornfield business. Had to be scary, huh?"

I shivered at the memory. Scary couldn't begin to describe it. Life-flashing-before-your-eyes terrifying was a more apt description. Fire coming from behind me as I knelt in the dirt, a gun aimed at my head, being sure I was going to die. I shivered again. *Get a grip*, Rational Me said.

I shook my head to clear it as the chief continued.

"Seriously, all quite impressive, Mackenzie. You did a great job there. Took real guts. Have you ever thought of joining the force? The department could use another sharp mind," he said, then added with a smile and a wink, "especially now that I've retired. Think about it, okay?"

I nodded and said nothing. As he walked away, I thought of all kinds of things I could have said, like, *Are you nuts? Me? A police officer? Not in a million years.*

Sure, I'd felt the adrenaline rush that comes with a brush with death, and part of me thought, for a crazy moment, that it felt good. But once I settled down, had a chance to think clearly again, I promised myself I'd never, ever get involved in another investigation. From now on, I'd only be investigating which shampoo was a better deal per ounce or which cell provider offered the best package. That's it. No more sticking my nose where it didn't belong.

I could have told Chief Bronson the truth, that the part I liked best about figuring out who killed Billy was when it was over. It was a one-and-done deal. I'd wanted answers for myself, for Billy, and for his family. But I'd put myself in harm's way, and now that I was home, safe and sound, I planned to stay that way.

I found Gram and Nathan just in time to hear Nathan's friend Jack say, "Cliff said he'd be here. Don't know what happened to him." He turned to Gram. "Cliff told us both last week at cribbage he was planning to come today. Don't know why he didn't show up."

Gram looked at me, a question in her eyes, which I interpreted as, *Maybe we should check and make sure Cliff is okay?* Which I knew meant that *I* would be the one doing the checking.

I telegraphed my answer: *Nope. My nosing around days are over. Not getting involved. Never again.*

# CHAPTER THREE

BACK HOME THAT AFTERNOON, I was headed to my room with Gram's copy of the latest China Bayles mystery when I heard Nathan yelling at Gram in their room down the hall. I knocked. "Everything okay in there?"

"Come in, Mackenzie," Gram said, then to Nathan, "Mackenzie is here now, so calm down."

He spat back. "Don't tell me to calm down! *You* calm down!"

Gram and Nathan glared at each other, seated on their respective twin beds with the matching blue and green plaid bedspreads. They both turned to me as I asked, "What's the problem?"

Nathan pointed at Gram. "It's her! She won't listen! Clark's in trouble. There's something wrong, and she won't do anything!"

Gram spoke, her tone flat and colder than I'd ever heard. "Nathan. Your brother Clark is dead. He died last year." She'd run out of patience.

Nathan furrowed his brow. "No, I just saw him at the senior center!"

Ah. Lightbulb. Gram softened. "Oh, you're talking about your friend Cliff, not your brother Clark?"

Nathan fixed her with a stare. "Why would I think Clark needs help? He's dead." He shot a glance at me, rolled his eyes, then turned back to Gram, speaking slowly as if explaining things to a child. "I'm talking about *Cliff.* Remember? Cliff Wilson? Jack said he's in trouble."

Gram sighed. "Jack just said he didn't know why Cliff didn't come to the ceremony. He didn't say anything about any trouble!"

Nathan scowled at her.

"Hey," I said. "I've got an idea. How about we call Cliff and see how he's doing?"

Nathan brightened. "Now you're cookin'!"

Gram opened the drawer in the bedside table and took out the ancient notebook where she keeps phone numbers. She found Cliff's number, then picked up the extension phone. (Yes. Extension phone. Landline. Gram doesn't have a cell phone and says she can't imagine ever needing one.)

Nathan and I waited as Gram punched in numbers, then held up fingers—one, two, three—as Cliff's number rang. Finally, an answer. Gram identified herself and asked, "Who am I speaking to?" She covered the phone with her palm and mouthed, "It's Jillian."

Gram asked to speak to Cliff, listened, then said, "Oh dear. Yes, I see. Please let us know how he's doing. Thank you."

Gram hung up. Nathan jumped to his feet. "I knew it! I knew it!" Then he jabbed a finger at Gram again and yelled, "How can she call? You didn't tell her our number!"

Gram stood, took his hand, and pulled him to sit next to her on his bed. She stroked the back of his hand, her voice soft. "It's okay, Nathan. She has the number. There's nothing to worry about, I'm sure, and Jillian—" She glanced at me. "Mackenzie knows Jillian, don't you, dear? Remember when she brought Cliff over last month?"

I said, "Oh, sure, I know her. Jillian's very nice." I turned to Nathan. "She and her brother take good care of Cliff."

Gram held Nathan's hand in both of her own. "It seems Cliff is in the hospital. I'm sure he'll be fine, and if you like, we can go visit him later."

"I told you he's in trouble! I'm going to go see him right now!" He started to stand again, but Gram pulled him back down.

"It's not visiting hours. We can go later. Let's take a little rest right now."

"I don't want to rest! I want to go see Cliff!"

Gram patted his hand again, then gently brushed his cheek and his forehead. After a few strokes, he visibly relaxed under her touch. She said, voice soft, reassuring, "I'm sure Cliff is fine, and he's probably sleeping right now. How about we take a little rest too?"

Nathan exhaled and lay back on his bed. Gram stood and draped a granny-squared afghan over him. He closed his eyes.

Gram turned to me, sighed. "I think I'll lie down for a bit too." She gave me a peck on the cheek as she ushered me out. "Thanks for your help, Sweetie."

I didn't think I'd been much help. Gram was doing all the heavy lifting in this house.

A minute later, settling onto the bed in the Rose Room, I tried to read, but my mind was on Gram. This caregiving thing she was doing seemed so hard, so scary. Like running a race, but you have no idea where the path will take you or where the finish line might be. But you know that when you get there, you'll have pain. Nathan would die. Gram would be alone—again. Widowed for the third time.

We'd talked about caregiving in the past, and Gram had said, "You become a better human being when you do for others."

"When have you sacrificed enough?" I'd asked.

"Sacrifice?" she said. "I don't see it that way. The Lord Jesus gave his life for me. Surely, I can do something so little for someone else."

"So *little*? What you're doing for Nathan is huge!"

She'd looked at me for a long moment. "Not huge, Sweetie. It's love. This is what those marriage vows mean—in sickness and in health. And I know, if needed, he'd do the same for me."

I wasn't sure Nathan could be there for Gram in the future, but in the here and now, I wanted to help her in any way I could. I resolved to make "sacrifices" for my grandmother, whatever that might mean.

I felt like a better human already.

# CHAPTER FOUR

'D GOTTEN THROUGH HALF a chapter in the China Bayles mystery when my brother Greg texted me. "Want to buy my car? Call me."

I called. Greg had recently bought himself a fairly new Ford F150 truck and was selling his fifteen-year-old Ford Escape. Cheap. How could I resist? An hour later, Greg was in Gram's driveway. His wife, Sarah, and the kids had followed him in her Expedition to give Greg a ride back home. They are a Ford family.

I looked the SUV over. The deep red paint job camouflaged the rust around the wheel wells. Tires were in decent shape. Long scrapes ran along the passenger side doors. "What happened?" I said, pointing at the scrapes.

"Close encounter with the garage. Had a little too much to drink that night."

I nodded. I knew that feeling—the too-much-to-drink, not the banging-into-things feeling. I sat in the Escape, hands on the wheel, looking at the dashboard.

Greg opened the passenger door. "Just had 'er tuned up. Tires are only a couple years old. Runs great. New battery too."

Sarah came to his side and looked in. "Sorry the car is such a mess." Indeed, the back seat was splattered with what I assumed were food stains, and empty fast-food containers littered most of the floor back there.

Greg draped an arm around his wife's shoulders. She sighed and said, "Greg, you could have at least cleaned the car. Now Mackenzie has to take care of your mess."

He shrugged. She shook her head and looked at me. "You know your brother."

"Indeed, I do," I said. The bedroom Greg shared with our younger brother, Robbie, in our childhood home was always a disaster. Greg blamed Robbie, and Robbie blamed Greg for the mess. I figured they were equally responsible.

The room I shared with little sister Deanne was always organized and neat. Little-touch-of-OCD Me took full credit for that.

Sarah went on. "And just a warning: our kids love collecting things—bugs, usually—when we're out and about. I can't guarantee that they all made it out of the car. I hope you don't find any dead things in there."

"Worse if they're alive!" I said. She laughed.

I laughed a little too soon.

*Chirrup. Chirrup.* The sound came from somewhere behind the back seat.

I looked at Greg. "What's that?"

"Oh yeah. Cricket."

*Chirrup. Chirrup.*

"Just one? Sounds like more."

"Hard to tell. I've tried to find it but couldn't. But don't worry. I'm sure once we have a hard freeze, it'll die."

*Chirrup. Chirrup.*

The car was in great shape, other than the trash and stains, both of which could be easily remedied. Greg made me an offer I couldn't refuse, as the saying goes, and I accepted. "No extra charge for the cricket," he said.

He and Sarah left, and I sat in my new-to-me car, engine running as I checked everything out. Lights, signals, horn, brakes. All good. I tapped the seat heater and a moment later, felt cozy warmth on my backside. I'd never had heated seats before.

I drove the Escape through town to Webster's Auto Repair. My poor old Chevy, Charlotte, had been sitting at Webster's for two weeks. The car had been charred by fire the previous month. Twice. Like me.

Charlotte was waiting for me to decide her fate: fix her or junk her. I checked her trunk and the glove compartment to be sure I hadn't left any valuables behind. Not that I had valuables. Everything smelled like roasted corn.

After a moment of silence, I pronounced Charlotte the Chevy dead and told Dan Webster to scrap her. Dan said he was feeling generous and gave me three hundred dollars for her.

I was sad to see Charlotte go—she and I had put on a lot of miles since I inherited her from sister Stephanie. But it felt good to have my own wheels again.

As I turned down Gram's street, I heard a chorus of chirps from behind the back seat, and then, it seemed, chirps coming from all directions at once. The warmer the car got, the more they chirped.

I parked behind the house and opened all four doors and the back hatch of the Escape.

Why is it so hard to find a cricket? When you go quiet to

try to figure out where they are, they go quiet. You give up. They chirp. Diabolical.

"Where are you, Jiminy?" I said.

*Chirrup. Chirrup.* Under the passenger seat. I looked. Nope.

"Yo! Jimbo!" Another chirp came from the back end of the car. Another from under the back seat. Then another from the driver's side. I went to one side of the car. Chirps came from the other side.

What do you call a bunch of crickets? A troop? A herd? No.

I decided this was an annoyance of crickets. Yes. Perfect.

Maybe I'd just wait for them to starve to death. Wouldn't take long once I removed the old french fries from the floor of the back seat.

Then I heard my friend Tansy, the meditation yoga guru, in my head, reminding me that the secret to inner peace is allowing what is to just be as it is. Or something like that.

Tansy has this amazing ability to, as she says, "accept all beings just as they are." That probably includes me, which is why we've been best friends since middle school.

Channeling Tansy, I said, "Okay, crickets. I accept that you are in this car." I took a deep breath. I felt calmer. *Maybe Tansy's onto something,* I thought.

But since my next thought was, *Please die soon,* I obviously had more to learn.

I closed the doors, hit the key fob. Chirp! The doors locked. I chuckled.

I named my new car Cricket.

# CHAPTER FIVE

I SAT AT THE KITCHEN table, enjoying a couple of Gram's amazing peanut butter cookies from her stash in the big hen-shaped cookie jar on the counter. Gram collects ceramic chickens. Her collection of a dozen sets of salt and pepper shakers—usually hens for the salt, roosters for the pepper—line the deep windowsill above her sink. Her cream pitcher is in the shape of a rooster, and the cream pours from his beak. A hen holds Gram's sugar.

A rooster painted on the wall clock keeps time. Pictures of poultry adorn her dish towels. A hand-sized plastic chicken has a scrub brush for its belly—especially handy for that dried egg yolk on a plate. Oh, the irony.

Chickens, chickens, everywhere.

Gram and Nathan came into the kitchen after their nap. Gram seemed calm.

Nathan was not. "Cliff's in trouble. Call him. Call him now!"

Gram pulled her phone directory from her sweater pocket, picked up the kitchen phone, and called Cliff's house again, talking with Jason this time. Hanging up, Gram said, "Jason said Cliff is still at Our Lady of Mercy."

Nathan was apoplectic. "Cliff needs help!"

Gram took his hand. "The doctors are taking care of him. Calm down."

Nathan jerked his hand away. "Don't tell me to calm down! I want to see Cliff! Now!" When Nathan got an idea stuck in his head and couldn't let it go, no amount of reasoning, subject-changing, or distraction seemed to work.

Gram sighed. "Okay, okay. We'll go see him right now." She turned to me, "Mackenzie, would you mind coming along? You can help Nathan into the hospital while I go park."

I pictured Gram trying to maneuver her big Buick through the labyrinth of the hospital parking structure. With arrows pointing every which way and tight turns, that ramp was confusing for anyone, let alone an elderly person under stress.

"It will be easier if I drop you both off. I'll park and meet you inside."

I traded my mom's sweatpants for a pair of jeans, and half an hour later, I dropped Gram and Nathan at the lobby door of Our Lady of Mercy. I parked in the hospital ramp, then took the elevator down to ground level and headed down a long corridor linking the ramp to the hospital.

A couple of weeks before, I'd spent a night in this hospital, recovering from nearly dying in "that cornfield business," as the chief called it. I walked faster and faster through the corridor, finally breaking into a trot.

Maybe I thought I could outrun the memories.

I couldn't.

Almost through the corridor, I heard an announcement. "Trauma Team One. Report to lobby. Trauma Team One. Report to lobby."

*Oh Lord. Gram? Nathan?* I'd been gone less than five minutes. What could have happened? I ran the rest of the way and skidded to a stop inside the lobby doors.

Several hospital personnel in scrubs were gathered around someone on the floor. My throat tight, my heart pounding, I squeezed in closer.

Nathan lay on the floor, looking dazed. I skirted around the group and found Gram standing, staring, speechless. Not like Gram at all.

I put my arm around her shoulders. She looked at me, eyes wide. She said, "He just collapsed. He said, 'I guess we should ask the waiter to take us to our table,' and then he just fell over. I tried to catch him, but he was too heavy."

"He thought you were at a restaurant?"

She looked at me. "I guess so. He's gotten worse, but this beats all." Yes, Nathan had seemed more confused and more irritable than usual lately.

Two men in scrubs arrived, one pushing a gurney. The medical team lifted Nathan onto it, and a female in purple scrubs turned to Gram. "You're a relative?"

"His wife, yes."

The nurse said, "We'll take him to the ER for assessment. Follow me." Gram and I trooped along behind the nurse, who walked behind the man pushing the gurney upon which Nathan lay, silent, eyes closed.

I thought, *This is the woman who followed the nurse, who followed the gurney . . .* remembering the children's story. *This is the dog that worried the cat that killed the rat that ate the malt that lay in the house that Jack built.*

# CHAPTER SIX

I N THE ER, GRAM and I sat in plastic chairs in the curtained space, waiting. Nathan lay silent on the bed. When Gram asked if he needed anything, he gave her a blank stare and said nothing. She asked again, "Are you okay, Nathan?" He frowned, closed his eyes, and turned his head away.

"Want me to get you a coffee, Gram?" She nodded, and I left her sitting beside the bed, holding Nathan's hand. When I returned, Nathan seemed to be asleep. Gram was crying softly. I sat next to her and put a hand on her arm. "Gram?" She was always so positive, so strong. I hated seeing her like this.

She looked at me and wiped at her eyes. "This is so difficult." The tears spilled. I pulled her close as she cried. I rubbed my hand along her back, felt her shoulder blades through her sweater. She'd lost weight, seemed fragile. A frailer version of my strong and capable grandmother.

She took a breath and wiped away the last tears with a tissue. She met my gaze. "I'm just tired. Don't worry about me. Where's that coffee?"

I handed her the Styrofoam cup. "I added cream for you. They only had half-and-half, not real cream." Gram loved to add whipping cream to her coffee.

"I can't taste the difference anymore," she said, resignation in her voice. Was she just tired? Depressed? Or was there something else going on with her?

A nurse in white and purple floral scrubs came into the cubicle. "Mrs. Powell, I'm Deborah. I'd like to get more information from you if I can." The nurse's voice had a calming quality, and Gram brightened just a bit.

Deborah crossed to the computer station on the other side of the bed. I stood to leave to give them some privacy, but Gram grabbed my arm. "Stay." I sat down again.

As Gram updated his medical history, Nathan lay mute, staring at the ceiling.

When the nurse asked, "Can you hear me, Nathan?" he stared at her. "Can you tell me your name?" More stares. Nothing.

Where the heck had Nathan gone, and how had he gone so quickly? His heart and respiration rates, displayed on the bedside monitor, seemed to be normal, steady. He had simply checked out.

After the nurse left, I whispered to Gram, "This is weird, isn't it?"

Gram nodded and said, a catch in her voice. "It's like he's just gone."

"Nathan has left the building," I said. Our family is like that, making jokes during awful moments. I hoped she'd smile.

She did then and repeated, her voice soft, "Nathan has left the building. Just like Elvis."

We sat sipping coffee. Deborah returned. "We'll be taking him for an MRI." She told Nathan the same thing. No response.

Gram spoke. "Have you seen this before? Doesn't it seem strange?"

"The doctor will let you know what he finds. This may take an hour or so. Maybe you'd like to get something to eat?"

I gave the nurse my cell number. She handed Gram a five-dollar cafeteria voucher and wheeled Nathan away.

# CHAPTER SEVEN

G RAM AND I TOOK the elevator to the basement cafeteria, where the voucher got us a plastic-wrapped turkey sandwich and a bag of Fritos to share. We munched in silence until I spotted a familiar face.

"Hey, there's Jillian." Jillian is hard to miss. Just shy of six feet tall, she has pale, almost translucent skin. Her long mane of strawberry blonde hair usually hangs down past her backside. Today she had it wound up on top of her head, adding another couple inches of bun to her height.

Gram looked up. "It's spooky how much she looks like her aunt Florence. And I feel bad now. I forgot about Cliff with all that's going on with Nathan." Gram waved Jillian over to our table and invited her to sit with us.

Every time I've seen Jillian—at Gram's when she's provided rides for Cliff or out and about town—she's been wearing the same basic thing. Plaid skirt, white blouse, and black and white saddle shoes with white knee-highs. That Catholic schoolgirl look is fine when you're fourteen. Not so much when, like Jillian, you're over forty.

Today, over the white blouse, Jillian had added a purple cardigan with a line of yellow and white daisies embroidered around the neckline. She'd buttoned the sweater all the way up to her chin and wrapped a coordinating purple and yellow scarf around her topknot.

Jillian sat, and Gram said, "That's a lovely sweater."

Jillian gave a shy smile and brushed her hand down the purple knit sleeve. "It's one of Aunt Florence's," she said. She touched the scarf atop her head. "So is this."

Gram smiled, "I thought it might be. I'm glad to see someone enjoying her beautiful things."

Jillian smiled a little wider and seemed to relax a bit. She leaned back into her chair, crossing her legs. Her plaid skirt slid up her leg, and I noticed a tattoo of a white owl on her right thigh, just above the knee.

"Cool owl tattoo," I said.

She tugged the skirt down. Her cheeks pinked, and she gave a shy smile. "It stands for purity and wisdom," she said. "Jason talked me into getting it years ago. He's got a black owl on his arm."

"So, if yours means purity and wisdom, what's the meaning of his?"

She gave a small chuckle. "The black owl means 'mystery and magic.' That's what the tattoo guy said. Jason thought that was cool."

The black owl seemed appropriate for Jillian's twin. Anytime I'd seen Jason, he was dressed in black. Even taller than Jillian, Jason was an imposing sight around town—well over six feet, black hair buzzed short, always looking like he needed a shave.

I was sure that as science teacher at the high school, Jason had no problems keeping his students in line.

Gram had told me that Jillian looked like their mother, Jean, and Jean's sister Florence. Jason resembled their father, who'd died in a car accident twenty years before. Their mother had died after a fall down the basement stairs just a few years back.

Jillian went on. "I didn't want my arm tattooed. The leg is not so obvious. Didn't want people staring or bugging me about it."

My turn to blush. "Oops. Sorry. I didn't mean to make you uncomfortable."

She waved off the apology. "No worries. I usually don't let it show." She shifted in her chair, adjusting the plaid skirt again.

Gram asked her what had happened to bring Cliff to the hospital.

Jillian stared off toward the cafeteria hot bar. "Uncle Cliff fell at home and hit his head on the fireplace hearth. I'm not sure how it happened. Maybe his dementia. Jason found him, and we called 911. He hasn't regained consciousness."

"How awful! He seemed to be doing fine lately," Gram said.

Jillian paused, then looked down at the table. "Well, he'd been having—I don't know what to call them—episodes, I guess. Dizziness, confusion. We just figured it was the dementia."

Gram and I exchanged a look. Cliff had seemed plenty sharp when he visited Nathan just a couple of weeks before. But I also knew that family caregivers often see a different picture than the occasional visitor sees and that things could change suddenly with age-related decline. Nathan was an example of that.

Jillian said she had to get back upstairs and left. When she was out of earshot, Gram said, "We just saw Cliff, and he was fine."

"Was he really? What about dizzy spells? Confusion?"

"I get dizzy sometimes too. Not such a big deal," Gram said.

"Maybe Cliff had a stroke. That can change things pretty dramatically, right?"

Gram shrugged. We finished the Fritos in silence, then headed back to the ER. A technician wheeled Nathan back to the cubicle a few minutes later.

It was after six that evening when the doctor came. Nathan was asleep. The doctor said, "The MRI didn't show anything new of concern since his last scan. We'll run some more tests, but meanwhile, we'll monitor him here overnight."

Gram thanked the doctor, and I offered to bring the car to the front entrance, but she said she wanted to walk with me to get it. She walked slower than her usual peppy pace.

"You okay, Gram?"

"Why do I feel so awful? I shouldn't feel so relieved that somebody else is taking care of him for the night. I'm a horrible person."

"You are not!"

"What if he wakes up and I'm not there? He might be scared or confused."

I stopped walking and took hold of her shoulders, turning her to face me. "He'll be *fine*. Someone will be there all night. Let the professionals take over while you get a good night's sleep. We'll come back tomorrow. Nothing to feel guilty about, Gram. You deserve a break."

She gave me a weak smile. "It's been a long day, kiddo," she said and then fell silent as we walked on.

It had been a long day, yes, on top of long weeks and months of caregiving. I held her hand and started skipping down the hallway, dragging her along as I sang, "We're off to see the wizard . . ." She laughed and joined in as we skipped our way to the elevator. She seemed in brighter spirits on the ride back to the Victorian, where she went straight to bed.

So did I.

# CHAPTER EIGHT

## Monday, November 12

G RAM WANTED TO GET to the hospital to check on Nathan early Monday morning. As we sat with coffee in her kitchen, she seemed tired—dark circles under her eyes, a slump to her shoulders. She's usually strong as an ox, stubborn as a mule—all the cliches fit my grandmother.

"You okay, Gram?"

She forced a wan smile and said, "Of course I am. Don't worry about me. *Sisukas!*" That Finnish word Gram learned from her Finnish grandmother, who'd come to America as a young girl in the early 1900s. The word meant that she had the mysterious quality Finns call *sisu*. "It means you keep on going, especially when things are tough," Gram always says.

She refilled our cups from her chicken-adorned electric percolator, adding a splash of whipping cream from the little rooster pitcher to both. We sat at the table.

"I'm fine," she said again. "I'm like that rabbit."

"Bugs?"

"No, you know. The whatchamacallit. Banging the drum."

"Ah, the Energizer Bunny."

"Yes! I take a lickin' and keep on tickin'!"

I didn't want to tell her she was mixing her advertising metaphors.

She sighed. "It's just always something as you get older. Now this, whatever this is, with Nathan. And whatever is going on with Cliff. Like we're all just falling apart on the way to death."

I didn't want to think about Gram being on her way out. "You've got a lot of years left, Gram. And you'll get through this. You always do. It's your *sisu*."

She fixed me with a stare. "Well, sisu or no sisu, sometimes you just get sick of having things to *get through*. I just wonder how much more I'm going to be able to take before I lose *my* marbles." She sipped her coffee. "Honestly, I didn't think I would survive after your grandfather died."

I smiled at the memory of Papa Powell, Gram's first husband. I was ten when he died in a work accident, a month before he'd planned to retire. No "golden years" in the cards for Papa and Gram.

Though she remarried twice after Papa died, Gram kept his last name. She was, and forever would be, "Virginia Powell, and I'm never changing my name for another man, not ever." Avantgarde for someone in her generation.

I admired that and kept my name after I married my late ex-husband. I have always been and will forever be Mackenzie Prentice.

Gram went on. "And then that situation with Chester—" Gram's second husband, a charming philanderer, had died of a massive coronary while *in flagrante* with a woman the family will forever call "The Hussy."

"That was awful," I said.

"But," she said, waving a hand above her head, "I wouldn't have all this if it hadn't been for Chester." She'd inherited the Victorian house and a whole lot of money from him. "And now, Nathan. He was so charming and so strong when we met on that cruise. We met dancing. Did you know that?"

I nodded. I'd heard the story many, many times but didn't say that, of course.

She looked away and sighed. "It was love at first samba, he always said." She smiled at me, reached out, and patted my hand. "I don't want to burden you with all my troubles. You've been through enough of your own lately."

I squeezed her hand. "Thanks for taking me in."

She smiled. "Families take care of each other. Ready to go?"

I nodded, and as I put our cups in the sink, my mother came into the kitchen. She'd started a new job at Lumber City Bank a few months back, helping people set up new accounts, apply for loans, and the like. With "a good head for numbers," she'd worked at various bookkeeping jobs in the past.

"How do I look?" she asked, twirling to model her white silk blouse, gray blazer, and navy slacks, and the french braid in her long ash brown, gray-streaked hair. Oversized square-framed glasses magnified her chestnut eyes.

I whistled. "Mom, you look great!"

She wrinkled her nose. "Do you really think I look okay? The bank has such a strict dress code. We have to look so professional all the time. Not even a casual Friday! Do I really look okay?"

Gram gave her a big smile. "You look gorgeous, Barbara. Relax, honey!"

Gram and I each gave her a hug, and I seconded Gram's opinion that the bank was lucky to have her. All the things you say.

We left her nervously picking lint off her slacks. Anxious. As always.

# CHAPTER NINE

OFFERED TO DRIVE GRAM to the hospital in Cricket. The chirping started as soon as we rolled down the alley, and as the car warmed up, the chirping increased.

"Sounds like you've got a whole orchestra of crickets in here," Gram said.

"Ah. Is that what you call them?"

"Yes. I learned that from the *New York Times* crossword. They're like little violinists, sawing away. *Orchestra* is appropriate, don't you think?"

"A noisy nuisance is what I think," I said.

To take my mind off the incessant chirping, I asked Gram about Cliff and Florence. They'd been frequent guests at each other's homes for dinner and game nights. "So much fun," Gram said. "Especially Florence. Great laugh. And Clifford absolutely adored her."

"She worked at Lambert's Grocery, right? I remember seeing her there."

"Yes, she was a cashier and then became a manager. But you know, she loved to write."

"Really? Did she ever get published?"

"Oh, she tried, but no luck. She gave up. She liked fooling around with words, was how she put it. She wrote in a journal, three pages every morning. She called them her *morning pages*."

Gram went on as I turned onto River Street. "Her sister Jean liked to write too. Florence and Jean exchanged letters, even though they both lived right here. I thought that was sweet, writing to each other like that. Letter writing is a lost art."

"Sad, isn't it? Florence gave up her dream."

"I think she liked the steady paycheck more." Gram lowered her voice and leaned toward me. "And Clifford didn't always work steady. It was hard for some men after the war."

We stopped at a red light on Fifth and River. I said, "I wonder where her journals are now. Wouldn't it be interesting to read them? Have you ever thought about writing about your life, Gram?"

"Heavens, no! The most writing I do is my grocery list. Can you imagine eighty years' worth of diaries? I'd need a warehouse to hold it all!"

"I'd love to have a record of your life, Gram. And to know what it was like for your grandparents." They were immigrants from Finland a century ago.

"It was hard," Gram said, her voice so quiet I could barely hear her over the crickets.

The light turned green, and I changed the subject. "That Jillian is quirky, huh?"

Gram laughed. "That's putting it mildly. Such an odd girl. And that brother of hers!"

42

"I remember seeing Jason's name on things in the high school trophy case. Science awards, I think."

"Yes, Florence always said he's a whiz. The high school is lucky to have him teaching there. Jillian's not a whiz at much. A nice enough girl, but I think she's always lived in Jason's shadow. Did you know them at school?"

"No, Gram, they're way older than I am."

Gram looked at me, appraising. "Of course. Silly me."

We parked in the hospital ramp. As we walked the corridor to the lobby, Gram asked, "What do you know about hoarding?"

"Not much. Just what I've seen on TV. Why?"

Gram explained that after Florence died, Cliff started collecting things. She and Nathan noticed, each time they visited, more and more stuff in the house. Eventually, Cliff stopped inviting them over.

"The last time we stopped by, he met us at the door with some excuse why he couldn't invite us in. I saw from the doorway that there were boxes everywhere. And it smelled awful in there." She sighed. "I worry about him."

"Did you talk to Jillian or Jason about it?"

"Jillian told me Clifford wouldn't allow her or her brother to touch anything. He gave them the upstairs of the house, but they had to leave his things alone. At least Clifford let Jillian clean the kitchen so she could cook. She told me she and Jason do what they can to be sure he's safe in the house."

"Doesn't sound like much of a life for any of them," I said. "Living in that kind of mess would drive me nuts." OCD Me shivered at the thought.

"Sad, really," Gram said. "Cliff's let the outside go, too, so Jason does the mowing and shoveling. I'm sure Cliff appreciates having them there."

"Sounds like a nice arrangement for everyone. They live rent-free, and Cliff has help." Like my mother, living at Gram's. And me too. I needed to talk to Gram again about how ridiculous it was for me, in my thirties, to be living rent-free at the Victorian.

Gram went on. "A nice arrangement, yes. But Cliff can be demanding too. We've assumed it's the grief. Once when Jillian came to pick him up from our house, he yelled at her, insisting he'd been waiting for hours! Called her stupid and inconsiderate. She was only a few minutes late, for goodness' sake. I thought the poor girl was going to cry. She looked so helpless, defeated." Gram paused, thinking. "Maybe Cliff *does* have dementia. Maybe he's worse than we thought."

"Hard to know what's going on," I said. I thought about Nathan snapping at Gram lately. And this latest episode at the hospital.

Gram said, "That day, after Cliff went out to the car, I asked Jillian if she was okay. She said she was fine, but I know how isolated caregivers can feel."

I felt a wave of compassion for Jillian. It was one thing to take care of a spouse or a parent. But a cranky old uncle? No thanks.

Gram continued. "Florence used to say that Jillian was a little slow. Just not very quick on the uptake. Not at all like her brother."

"Jillian must have something on the ball. She works at Lumber City Bank, right? Mom said they often work the same hours."

"Yes, Jillian's been a teller for years, and I'm sure she's competent at her job. I think it's just socially that she's a little awkward."

We reached the lobby, and before going to Nathan's room, we stopped at the information desk to ask about Cliff's condition. Since we weren't family members, they couldn't tell us anything. We were waiting for the elevator when the elevator door opened, and Jillian came out, looking distracted.

Gram spoke. "Jillian? How's your uncle?"

Jillian stared at Gram, then me, as if she were trying to figure out who we were. Then she shook her head. "Oh, it's you. Uncle Cliff is—uh, he just died."

Gram laid a hand on Jillian's arm and started to say, "I'm so sorry—"

Jillian pushed the hand away, looking past us. "I have to find Jason," she said.

I said, "Let us know—" but Jillian was already hustling away. As we rode the elevator, I said, "That was rude."

"Probably just in shock. Let's not mention this to Nathan," Gram said.

We walked into Nathan's room. The doctor was there, and Nathan seemed to be his old self, smiling, listening, and responding appropriately. The doctor probably had no clue that anything they'd just discussed would likely be forgotten.

The doctor looked at me and explained that Nathan had a urinary tract infection. "Very common cause of confusion in the elderly. I've prescribed a course of antibiotics," he told me. He must have assumed I was the caregiver for both Gram and Nathan.

I pointed at Gram. "This is his wife. Tell her."

"Sorry," the doctor said, then turned to Gram and started talking slower and a little louder, treating Gram like some feeble old woman. I wanted to slug him. "I've prescribed antibiotics. You can pick that up in the pharmacy downstairs."

Gram didn't seem to notice the condescension. She just nodded and then asked, "What about the way he just checked out? Was it a stroke?"

Since Nathan had come out of it, and the tests they'd done hadn't shown any evidence of stroke, just the UTI and dehydration, the doctor called it a "transient alteration of consciousness."

"What causes that?" Gram asked.

"We don't know," the doctor said. "It just happens sometimes."

"Will it happen again?" Gram asked.

The answer: "Can't say for sure."

Gram and Nathan took the back seat on the way home. I heard her explaining things to him—with cricket orchestra accompaniment. She repeated the doctor's words. "'Don't know, can't say'? What good are they?"

Nathan laughed out loud, a welcome sound after the silence and disconnect. "It's a poem! Don't know, can't say, what good are they? What good are they?"

They repeated the phrases together, laughing as they held hands in the back seat.

The bad news about Cliff would definitely keep.

# CHAPTER TEN

NATHAN AND GRAM HEADED upstairs after lunch to rest. Just as I finished eating, Vince Hampton called my cell. Vince is the fire investigator for Three Rivers Fire and Rescue. He'd been on the scene after my apartment was firebombed the previous month.

I'd met Vince when I was in seventh grade. He was in ninth grade, a friend of my older brother Greg's. Vince had curly brown hair and hard-to-resist honey-brown eyes with flecks of amber. "A heartbreaker," my mother called him. I was willing to let him break mine, anytime.

Vince used to tease me, turning my given name, Mackenzie Annabelle, into "Macaroni Banana-Belly." I pretended to be annoyed while, of course, secretly loving his attention.

Vince, who I'd heard was divorced, had asked after the fire if I'd like to go out sometime. I'd agreed and, when he called, my little heart went all pitty-pat. *Me and Vince—going out at last.*

My little heart went pitty-phffft when Vince explained, "I'm calling to see if you want to go to your apartment to see what you can salvage. If you're ready to see it, that is."

The fire, in the middle of the night, had left me with my pajamas, robe, wallet, flip-flops, cell phone, and my parakeets, Tweet and Chirp. That and a few emergency supplies I had in a suitcase in the trunk of my car. Everything else, I expected, was gone.

Vince reminded me that, because the fire damage had revealed that the duplex likely had an asbestos problem, I'd need a hazmat suit and an escort. He offered to provide both. Not the most glamorous of first dates, but Lonely Me wasn't going to be picky.

We drove to my former duplex in his metallic blue Chevy Silverado. Vince and my brother Greg had an ongoing debate. Ford versus Chevrolet. Whose trucks delivered greater stud-power? Boys and their toys.

We suited up on the sidewalk outside my former residence, looking like astronauts in the white paper suits, gloved and booted, with our faces hidden by goggles and respirators. The place looked absolutely normal if you ignored the yellow CAUTION DO NOT ENTER tape across the front door. Surreal.

Vince held the tape aside as I unlocked the front door, using the spare key I'd given my mother. We stepped into the living room. My drapes were still hanging, blocking out the daylight. We switched on our flashlights. I took in the scene. We'd entered a different dimension, crossed into alien territory, landed on some other planet.

"Holy crap," I managed to say. "What a stench!" The respirator did little to stop the noxious odors. Vince explained that in a structure fire like this, the heat and smoke go into the walls, furniture, fabrics, and floors. "It goes anywhere air can go. And it doesn't stop when the flames are out." As the scene cools, bad stuff continues to be released, he said. My stomach churned, and I swallowed hard. I had no desire to puke in my mask.

I looked around. Sagging drapes. Water-soaked couch. Laptop on the coffee table, no doubt beyond repair. I wiped a gloved finger across the table and came up with black slime.

"Water damage everywhere," Vince said, pointing at the floor. The old hardwood had warped in spots, and dark stains crept up the walls from the baseboards. "Gonna be a total gut," he said. I felt gutted too.

Vince led the way into the kitchen at the back of the apartment, where the fire had started. Cupboards destroyed. Laminate countertop rippled and charred.

I felt a crunch underfoot and shone the light down on granola, Cap'n Crunch, and Froot Loops. Someone had dumped it all out, tossing the boxes to the side. The drawer where I kept my extra cash—usually less than fifty bucks—was on the floor, emptied.

"Vince, somebody's been in here." I pointed at the cereal. Snarky Me whispered, *Ooh, somebody's been eating your cereal? Goldilocks maybe?*

Vince shrugged.

"No, seriously! Someone's been here, looking for something. People on TV hide valuables in coffee cans and in cereal boxes all the time. Crooks know this!"

He laughed and air-quoted. "Ooh, a *crook*, huh? How would this, uh, *crook*, get in? Everything's been locked up. The caution tape was intact."

"Do you think a little piece of plastic tape is going to stop a bad guy?"

"Why would they break in? Did you *have* something valuable stashed here? And how did they get in? The front door was locked. The windows aren't broken. The back door and that window—" He gestured to the window above the sink. "—are covered with plywood."

I hollered, "They could have taken the plywood off the back door and then put it back!"

Vince held up a hand. "Okay, okay. Take it easy. We can go out there and check."

"I want to see what else they stole. Let's check the bedroom," I said.

He bumped his shoulder into my arm. "Anything you say, Macaroni." His eyes held the smile obscured by his respirator. He waggled his eyebrows, which wiggled his goggles.

I slugged him in the shoulder. "Don't be such a perv!" He gave a muffled laugh.

I pointed my flashlight and, with Vince following, led the way into the bedroom. The bed was soaked and probably growing all sorts of interesting fungi, thriving in the dark and the damp.

"Nice waterbed," Vince said with another eyebrow wiggle. I slugged him again.

I opened my closet door. Let's be honest. I didn't care about the couch, the drapes, or the bed. I just wanted my clothes. A girl can only borrow from her mother and grandmother for so long.

I particularly wanted my favorite shirt. I'd owned the long-sleeved cotton shirt since college. Loved its muted blue and green plaid. It was my go-to with jeans in chilly weather. A soft layer under a sweater in winter. The perfect shirt, its only flaw a tiny ink stain on the right sleeve.

The closet was stripped clean. The shirt was gone, along with my shoes, my UGG knockoffs, and my Katy Perry boots that cost half a month's pay and killed my feet but looked oh-so-cute. (Ah, the price we pay for fashion.)

Gone. All gone. Also gone were the jeans, sweaters, and sweatshirts I'd left folded on the shelf. That included the blue sweatshirt my ex-boyfriend, Kyle-leaving-me-for-Bangladesh, wanted back. He'd cared more about his sweatshirt than my safety after the fire. I'd have to text him, Kyle-style: *SRE. BLU SWTSHRT STOLN. 2BAD JRK!* Or something like that.

I clumped over to my three-drawer dresser. Empty. "They took my underwear! Who *does* that? What kind of a sicko steals your underwear?"

I swept the flashlight beam to the jewelry box on my bedside table. The top lid stood open. My heart sank. Earrings and necklaces gone, which was no big deal—most of them I'd bought at Target. Nothing precious in my jewelry collection, with one exception. One thing that meant something to me.

A diamond brooch given to Gram by her mother, passed to my mother when she married my father, and then given to me on my wedding day since I was the first of my sisters to get married. Not actual diamonds, of course—we're not *that* family. It's a copy of a brooch owned by someone related to the British royal family. Lady Somebody or Countess Something.

About two inches in diameter, the brooch has wavy lines of rhinestones and looks pretty real if you don't know the facts. It sparkles like heck and is the only thing in the family that qualifies as an heirloom. Even though I never wore it and didn't expect I ever would, I wanted it.

My voice shook as I described the pin to Vince. Tears spilled. Everything—the brooch, my clothes, the fire damage—suddenly felt overwhelming. I yelled as I cried, "I've been robbed! Definitely robbed!"

Crying is a very messy proposition when you're wearing PPE.

Vince steered me by the elbow out of the bedroom and then out the front door. Standing on the front sidewalk, he took off his mask and goggles. I did likewise, sniveling and gulping down my sobs as I did so. He went to his car and came back with a wad of paper towels. "Here. Blow."

I blew, took a few deep breaths, and cleared my head.

"Better?" he asked.

"Uh-huh." I took a few more breaths, feeling calmer with each one.

We peeled off the paper hazmat suits and booties. Vince shoved them into a black garbage bag, adding our gloves last. Then he turned to me. "You think you were robbed, huh? I don't see how. No sign that I can see of anyone breaking in."

"We haven't checked the back," I said and headed around the building, Vince in tow.

# CHAPTER ELEVEN

ROUNDING THE CORNER, I saw what was left of the back of the building where the fire had started. My knees buckled. Vince grabbed me and held me up as I looked up at the blistered siding.

I could see Mrs. Litowsky's kitchen window upstairs, directly above mine. Her philodendron, withering, still hung above her kitchen sink. Mrs. Litowsky had to go live with her sister. I was at Gram's. Our lives had been upended. How can someone do that to someone else? I felt a wave of anger and, a moment later, a cold chill of fear.

Anxious Me whispered, *If this could happen once, it—or something even worse—could happen again.* I'd had enough fiery encounters in the past month to last a lifetime.

"You okay?" Vince asked.

I nodded and took a step toward what was left of the back porch. I looked down at my feet. *This is where I was standing right before I was pushed down.* My hand found the tender spot near my right eye, where my face had smacked the burnt wood of the step. The bruise on my cheekbone was now a lovely shade of greenish yellow. *Here I fell.* I looked at my left hand where the shard of glass pierced the flesh. The stitches in my palm had finally dissolved. My hand still hurt.

As I stood reliving the memories, Vince checked the plywood covering the back door and window of my apartment. "Look at this," he said. I stepped onto the porch. "The window is secure, but look there," he said, pointing at several screws lying on the porch floor. He wiggled the plywood over what used to be my back door. It came away from the wall easily.

I said, "That plywood was screwed in place before, when I came back for my car. I know it was. Someone—"

Vince finished the thought as he nodded. "Yep, someone broke in." He looked at me then, something shifting in his eyes. "But why? Why would someone break into *your* place? Anything you're not telling me?"

I didn't like the note of suspicion in his voice. "What the hell? Are you accusing me of something?"

"Of course not. I'm just wondering why someone would break into *your* place. You're not exactly rich. You didn't have a lot of fancy electronics or expensive toys, did you?"

"What? Are you saying I'm not *worth* robbing?" I stopped, recognizing the absurdity in what I'd just said. Vince chuckled. I slugged him in the arm. He pretended it hurt.

I went on. "Maybe they *thought* I had money. Maybe they thought they were breaking into someone else's place. How should *I* know what *they* thought?" My voice rose louder with every word. "I just don't understand why they'd take my clothes! Who *does* that?"

"Maybe they were just after jewelry and took the clothes as an afterthought."

"None of the jewelry had any value, except for the brooch, and that's just sentimental. I'm really sad that's gone."

We both went quiet. The people who set this fire were in jail. They couldn't have come back to rob me or to cover up any evidence of arson. I voiced this aloud, and Vince agreed.

"Nothing to cover up," Vince said. "They used kerosene and a match. Simple."

"Simple? No. They destroyed my life. Nothing simple about that!"

"Of course," he said. "I just meant there's nothing to try to cover up. It's obvious what happened here." I only half-listened as he went on to explain how challenging arson investigations could be since evidence is often destroyed in the fire. "But traces of an accelerant will always be there. It's just a matter of having the equipment needed to find it." And Vince did.

He continued. "I concluded that your kitchen window was the point of access. Must have been unlocked, or did you maybe leave it open?"

My heart sank. I sucked in a breath. "I did have that window open that day. It was such a warm afternoon. I don't remember closing it when I went to bed."

"So, the arsonist tears off the screen," he said, pointing at the twisted frame of the window screen in the side yard. "Then reaches in the open window, pours kerosene inside, and dumps the rest on the porch under the window. Tosses a match, and whoosh!" He snapped his fingers.

I winced. I pictured my open window, kerosene flowing onto the countertops, the floor. Me, sound asleep, Tweet and Chirp in their cage, Mrs. Litowsky asleep upstairs—all of us oblivious to the scumbag just twenty feet away who was about to turn our lives upside down. I shivered.

55

"You okay?" Vince asked again. I shook my head. Thinking about the what-ifs and worst possible scenarios sapped me. Even though I'd survived, Anxious Me kept replaying the danger.

Vince went on. "Whoever broke in after the fire may have been looking for drugs, or cash, or anything else they could hock." He smiled. "And they took your clothes 'cuz they liked your style." His joke fell flat.

I scowled. "So now I'm going to look at every random person on the street, wondering if they're wearing my underwear?" With that thought, anger rose again. "Well, whoever it is, I hope they enjoy my stuff. Just give me my damn shirt and the damn brooch! Keep the rest, you rotten son of a—!" I was going to start bawling again any second.

"Hey, hey, hey," Vince said, arm around my shoulders.

"It's fine. I'm fine. Fine," I lied, my voice a little squeaky. I couldn't stop trembling. Someone out there right now was pawing through my stuff. A wave of emotion swamped me. Anger. Disgust. Sadness. Anxiety. Fear. Powerlessness. Anger again.

Maybe this was post-traumatic stress. Maybe I needed to call Dr. Angela, the psychologist, again. She'd helped me before when I was adjusting to my divorce. Maybe I needed a little more adjustment.

Vince pulled me into a hug and said, "It'll be okay." My ear pressed against his chest. I felt his warmth. I heard his heart beating as his voice rumbled, deep and soothing. "It'll be okay," he repeated until my trembling became shivering and then stopped altogether. Finally, I let out a huge breath, and he released me.

I sat down on the porch steps, eavesdropping as Vince called my former landlord, telling him—no, *ordering* him in his official arson investigator's voice, which gave me a nice little shiver of a different kind—to come immediately and make sure the premises were secure.

My ex-landlord must have argued about it because I heard Vince say something about "attractive nuisance" and "potential lawsuit." Very official and very sexy.

Vince and I walked to the front of the building. I locked the front door, and just as I opened the passenger door of Vince's Silverado, I heard a meow. I looked down.

Chloe.

With her brilliant green eyes and black and white striped fur, Chloe belonged—if cats ever actually belong to humans—to Mrs. Litowsky. She hung out with Mrs. L when the weather was wet or cold. The rest of the time, she was an outside cat. She'd graced me with her presence at times when Mrs. L was gone.

I'd thought about Chloe many times after the fire, hoping she was okay, wondering how awful she might have felt, coming back to nothing, to nobody. Mrs. L had called me to ask if I'd seen her and told me she'd come by the duplex every day to leave a bowl of cat food outside. Every day, the bowl was empty, but, of course, she couldn't be sure who ate it.

And now Chloe had come home. She wound herself around my calves, purring. She let me pick her up. I felt honored. She usually avoided human touch.

When we were in the truck, I said, "Vince, meet Chloe." I waved her paw. "Chloe, this is Vince. He's a good human."

Vince's cheeks reddened. "Um, nice to meet you, um, Chloe." Cute, that blush. He started the engine. "What are you going to do with her? Call animal control?"

"Absolutely not! I'll call Mrs. Litowsky and see what she wants to do. I can keep her at Gram's if necessary."

As we drove, I called Mrs. L on my cell. "Thank Gott she's safe!" she said, in her slight German accent. She explained that, much as she'd love to take Chloe, the sister she was staying with was allergic to cats. "Gif her a good home, von't you?"

I assured Mrs. Litowsky that I would. And that's how Chloe came to live with me. And my two birds. And my mother. And my grandmother. And Nathan.

Another snippet of children's rhyme popped into my head, which I recited aloud, making patty-cake with Chloe's paws, ending with, "He had a crooked cat, who caught a crooked mouse, and they all lived together in a crooked little house!"

Vince's look implied that he questioned my sanity. I smiled as Chloe purred on my lap.

At my request, we made a quick detour to Pudasek's Hardware—more a general store than just nuts and bolts. I bought cat essentials and a couple of toys, including a toy mouse on wheels stuffed with catnip "guaranteed to drive your cat wild with delight."

Too bad they don't make that kind of thing for humans. Or maybe they do, and I've just never owned one.

Vince helped me carry things into the house. He gave me strict instructions, in that official investigator voice of his, to take a shower, just in case any asbestos or other creepy stuff was clinging to me.

"Make it a long . . . hot . . . shower," he said, his voice quiet as he looked at me with those heartbreaker amber eyes. I held my breath. Waited.

With a look that said he knew the effect he was having on me, he broke eye contact, smiled, and said, "You got it?"

I gave him a salute. "Yes, sir!"

He grinned. "Let's do this again?"

"What? Go through an arson scene?"

"No. How about a real date next time, Banana-Belly?"

I blushed like a middle-schooler. I stammered and tripped over my tongue. "Yeah, sure, um, Prince Vince." Okay, so I suck at improv.

"*Prince*, huh? I like it. Suits me, don't you think?"

I shoved him in the shoulder. "Yeah, because you're a royal pain."

He laughed. "See ya!" he said and trotted out to his truck.

*Way to keep your cool,* Snarky said. I told her to shut up.

I held Chloe, scratching behind her ear as we watched the Silverado disappear down the block. Even though the apartment was a complete loss with nothing to salvage, at least I knew where I stood—solidly in the starting-over-from-scratch zone. At least I had the money my ex had left me.

"You're starting over too, huh, Chloe?" I whispered into her fur as I hugged her. Her coming back felt like a sign. She was okay, and maybe I'd be okay too.

*Yes, maybe,* Hopeful Me whispered.

# CHAPTER TWELVE

V INCE'S TRUCK WAS OUT of sight. Gram and my mother came down the stairs as I turned from the front door. My mother frowned. Gram smiled. "And who is this sweet little one?" She stroked Chloe under the chin. The cat closed her eyes.

I gave them the highlights of Chloe's history, ending with, "If it's okay, we now have a cat."

"What do you mean *we*?" my mother said. "I hate cats. Never had one, never wanted one, and never will!"

"Geez, Mom, how do you really feel?" Chloe bristled and stiffened in my arms. I set her down, and she rubbed against Gram's leg with a loud purr of approval.

Chloe followed us into the dining room. When I sat down, she jumped into my lap, curled up, and settled in. My mother, seated as far as she could away from us, gave a grunt of disgust.

Gram reached over and rubbed Chloe's ear. "Poor kitty. She must have been so scared out there."

"She's used to being outside," I said, "but I'm sure she was confused when she came back and nobody was there. And she's never been this friendly before."

My mother made another noise. "Ugh. You never know what an outside animal is bringing into the house. Just keep it away from me!"

"She has a name, Mother. This is Chloe."

"I'm not about to get attached." She jabbed a finger in the cat's direction. "As far as I'm concerned, that *thing* is an *it!*" She spit the word out.

"Whatever, Mom. I'm sure if you got to know her—"

"Don't start. I'm never going to *get to know* any stupid cat."

Chloe stopped purring, her ears flicked, and she stared at my mother. My mom stared back. After a few seconds, Chloe lowered her head and closed her eyes. *Advantage, Barbara.*

Gram spoke. "Well, she can certainly stay here, poor darling."

My mother glared at Gram. "Don't we have enough to deal with around here?"

I assumed she meant Nathan. Gram looked as if steam were about to come out of her ears. She glared back, then spoke, her words chopped. "Don't—you—*dare* tell *me* we have too much to deal with around here. We're a family! We take care of each other! And now another little lost soul needs our help. Stop being so . . . so selfish!"

I'd never heard Gram talk to my mother, or anyone else, that way. My mom looked shocked, cleared her throat, and hung her head. "I'm sorry, Mother."

*Wow.* My mom didn't argue. She'd gone passive. *Advantage, Gram.*

Gram's tone softened. "Barbara, I'm sorry I snapped. You've been such a help with Nathan and everything. I'm thankful you're here." Gram turned to me. "I'm glad you're here too, Mackenzie." Then she patted Chloe's head. "And you too, little kitty."

This was turning into quite the love fest. I expected we'd all be purring in a second.

Later, Chloe curled by my side on the bed in the Rose Room. I'd checked her over and found no bumps, bruises, cuts, or scrapes. I called Mrs. Litowsky again. She assured me Chloe was up to date on her shots and spayed long ago. Excellent. I didn't think my mother could tolerate a litter of kittens.

Chloe was fine physically, but something in her spirit had changed. Maybe too many nights stuck outside had cured her wanderlust. As if, now that she'd found me, she wasn't going to leave me.

When Chloe wasn't on my bed, she curled up in a sunny spot in the room Gram called the front parlor, which just happened to be where the birdcage was. I preferred to think that she wanted to be near the birds because she sensed that Tweet and Chirp were part of me and not that she hoped they'd become part of her, as in lunch.

Nice as it was to be Chloe's human, I didn't know where I was heading next in life. I might decide to move far away. Maybe Tahiti. I didn't need any extra encumbrances.

But Gram didn't need another living being to take care of. And I was sure my mother would throw a hissy-fit if I left Chloe behind.

Chloe closed her eyes, purring under my hand. I whispered, "Okay, girl, if I leave, you come with me." She opened her eyes and gave me a look that clearly said, *Well, duh.*

# CHAPTER THIRTEEN

Tuesday, November 13

UESDAY MORNING, I WAS enjoying eggs and bacon with Gram. My mother came into the kitchen, dressed for work. She poured herself a cup of coffee and sat at the table.

She glanced from me to Gram, then lowered her voice. "You have to swear you won't tell anyone what I'm about to tell you." Gram and I exchanged a glance, then nodded.

"I'm serious. Promise? I could lose my job if you say anything."

She definitely had our attention.

She took a breath and looked at Gram. "A few weeks ago, that Jason brought your friend Cliff into the bank. Jillian works there, you know?" We nodded. "The three of them came to me and said that Cliff wanted to add them both to his accounts. I asked Cliff if he was sure about that, and he nodded. His hands shook so badly, I asked if he was all right. He nodded again.

"Then Jillian asked if I could get him a glass of water. I left to get it, and when I came back, the paperwork was signed to put his accounts in all three of their names. I asked Cliff again if that's what he wanted, and he said yes. Families do that kind of thing all the time, but now that Cliff is gone, well, I'm just wondering about the whole thing."

Gram said, "But it makes good sense, doesn't it? If I was all alone, I'd want one of you on my financials, just in case. In fact, I should set that up now. It's so much easier that way for the family."

I felt that pang again, thinking about Gram not being around anymore.

Gram went on. "Cliff and Florence had the house, of course. But she worked at the grocery store, and he was a bus driver for a time, then worked construction. I think her only indulgence was her Chanel perfume. She did love her Chanel."

I piped up. "His bank accounts couldn't amount to much, right? Maybe just enough to bury him?"

My mother looked to the left and right as if making sure nobody else could hear us. She leaned forward and whispered, "I can get fired for telling you this, but he had over a hundred grand in his accounts."

Gram and I both sat back in our chairs. Gram said, "Geez, Louise!"

I let out a whistle. "Wowzers! Where did that come from?"

My mother shrugged. "I have no idea. I checked, and it was just sitting there in his checking account for several years, earning interest."

"Florence must have had life insurance," Gram said.

"That would explain it," I said.

My mom looked worried. "Please promise you won't tell anyone?"

I crossed my heart. Gram did that little lip-locking move

and threw away the pretend key. "I'm trusting you both," she said and left for work.

Gram said, "Well, don't that beat all? That's a lot of simoleons!"

"Mucho dinero!" I said.

"Whole lotta loot!" Gram said. We spent the next couple of minutes calling it cabbage, bread, dough, moolah, smackers, cheddar.

I laughed and said, "Okay, enough! It's a lot of clams!"

"Darn. Now I'm hungry for chowder," Gram said as she went upstairs to wake Nathan.

I tossed the last bit of my bacon to Chloe and put my plate in the sink. I poured another cup of coffee and sat at the table, thinking about Jillian and Jason finagling their way onto Cliff's bank accounts. And now he was dead.

Gram and Nathan came downstairs. I made eggs and toast for Nathan while Gram used the kitchen phone to check on Cliff's funeral arrangements. She hung up and sat with us at the table, scowling.

"I can't believe it. No funeral. No service at all. Awful. Just awful. So sad. A person lives their whole life, and there's nothing to mark their passing. What are those kids thinking? I just don't understand it."

"Who told you that?"

"Jillian. She didn't seem to have a clue about what we do when someone passes. She's such an awkward little thing."

*Awkward, for sure, but six-foot-tall Jillian is hardly 'little.'*

Gram brightened and said, "Maybe someone could do something at the senior center, or the VFW."

"Can that be done if the family doesn't want it?" I asked.

"I can sure find out and make a few calls. Somebody should do something for poor Clifford. Such a nice man."

Nathan piped up. "Cliff? Yep, he's a great guy. Saw him just the other day. We should have him over."

"Eat your eggs, dear," she said. He dug in.

Gram looked at me. "I feel awful. Cliff and Florence were such good friends of ours. And since Florence died and those two moved in, it's just never been the same with him. Something has just not been right."

"Like what, Gram?"

Gram has a keen ability to read people and situations. She'd been able to tell if one of us kids had a fever just by looking at us. She'd diagnosed strep throat more than once, just by noticing dark circles under our eyes. Doctor confirmed. Yes, strep.

She credited her keen intuition to her almost nine decades of experience. "Well, sometimes Cliff seemed so distracted when he came over, like he was here but not here, but I'm sure that was his grief at losing Florence. But then, over time, he was better. And now he's gone. He was fine. And now he's gone." She snapped her fingers.

"He wasn't exactly *fine*, Gram. Dizzy spells, remember? In the hospital a few times in the past year. Not really fine."

"You know, Florence told me she had concerns about those kids. Florence said her sister, Jean—their own mother—had concerns too."

"What kind of concerns?"

"Oh, she never said anything specific, just that something wasn't quite right. No details. Just something."

I pictured Jillian dressed like an overgrown schoolgirl and Jason with the Man in Black look. "Maybe they just have their own style. Quirky non-conformists?"

Gram shrugged. "I guess so, but it seemed there was something else." Her eyes widened. "Do you suppose you could—?"

"Could I what?" I asked, wishing immediately I hadn't said it. I knew how this would go. Gram would say she had a funny feeling about Cliff's death. She'd ask me to check into things.

I'd want to tell her absolutely not, no way, never again, in no uncertain terms. That I didn't want to end up beaten, or burned, or worse. That we should leave it to the police to figure out if something bad happened. Not my business. Not my job. Not my concern. Nope. Never again.

But then she'd look at me with her little blue eyes in her little cherub face, giving me a sad smile. She'd say she knows it's a lot to ask but that she thinks I'm so smart and that she'll be able to sleep so much better if I would just check and make sure nothing awful happened to Cliff.

And I'd end up saying yes to Gram because, well, it's Gram. Gram asks you to do something, you do it.

I decided to save us both some time. "Do you want me to do some checking? See if there's any reason to think this was something other than the obvious?"

She smiled a huge grin, her little eyes disappearing into her cheekbones as she laid one hand to her cheek. "Oh, I wish I'd thought of that!"

*Seriously? Did she think I'd buy that?*

She hugged me. "That would be wonderful, Mackenzie! You're such a clever girl, and I'll sleep better knowing everything is fine."

I swear the old woman can read minds.

"I'll do some checking, but I'm sure I'll find that Cliff got dizzy, fell, hit his head, and died. End of story."

Gram said, "Sweetie, I sure hope you're right."

I hoped so too.

# CHAPTER FOURTEEN

M Y OLDER SISTER, STEPHANIE, showed up unexpectedly later Tuesday afternoon. She lives and works in The City, a couple of hours from Three Rivers. She comes to visit for holidays and other family events but doesn't just drop in.

"Mom called me. I have something for you out in my car." I took one of Gram's jackets from the hook in the entryway and followed my big sister outside toward the sleek blue Jaguar at the curb, its finish sparkling like sapphires in the morning sun.

I let out a low whistle. "Nice car," I said.

Snarky whispered, *She's got a Jag. You've got crickets.*

The contrast between my car and Stephanie's is a perfect metaphor for us as sisters. Stephanie, oldest of my siblings—with an MBA and a fabulous career as a big city investment adviser. Me, the middle kid—with a bachelor's in psychology and no career, living with my granny in our little town.

Steph, never married, is currently "keeping company," as Gram says, with a wealthy widower, twenty years her senior, named Mason Wyborn. She insists it's not about his money. She has enough of her own. "He makes me laugh," she says. "We have fun."

They have Cabo fun. Turks and Caicos fun. Private plane to Paris for dinner fun.

By contrast, I have living-with-my-grandmother and having my underwear stolen by some low-life kind of fun.

And now here she was, with her shiny new Jag. As I opened the passenger door to admire the interior, she explained. "Got it as a bonus for exceeding my goals this year. Sweet, huh?"

"Mmm-hmmm," I said, trying not to drool on the leather. I ran my hand over the passenger seat. "Like butter," I said.

"Baby's bottom," she said. I tried to imagine a job with such perks. What did I get from my former boss, Trip Kipling? Well, most recently, a pink slip. Before that, last Christmas, he handed me a basket of assorted cheeses, which I suspect was a regift. It's the thought that counts, right? And in this case, he gave me no thought whatsoever.

"Come back here," Steph said, key-fobbing the trunk open. I looked in at several white plastic trash bags. "Mother said you lost everything in that fire, so I cleaned out my closet. I had a few extra things I thought you could use."

Stephanie cleaned out her closet? My heart did a little flip as I imagined myself with new best friends in my closet named Giorgio, Dolce, Gabbana, and Gucci. *Oh, the fanciness of it all!*

We carried the bags into the house. On the way up to the Rose Room, Steph asked, "Why don't you just buy some new clothes? Mom said you got some money from Billy."

I didn't want to tell her that I preferred not to spend that money until my future was a little more certain. She'd probably think I was silly and try to talk me into investing in something.

I said, "I hate shopping for clothes." That was true. I had never really found a sense of my own style. Hand-me-downs from Stephanie, or worse, from big brother Greg, had been much of my wardrobe all through school.

She nodded. "You do seem to go with jeans and tees and sweatshirts. Maybe it's time to expand a little."

"Hey, I had a pair of black pants and a nice blazer, too, before they were stolen."

She gave me a look. "Yeah. Whatever," she said as she emptied the first bag onto the bed. "Maybe there's something here you'll like."

I felt a tingle, anticipating designer wonderfulness. Nope. "It's sweats," I said.

She corrected me. "Athleisure."

Whatever. Not a designer label in the bunch.

The next bag was socks and pajamas, mostly flannel. *C'mon, where's the good stuff?* I chuckled, thinking of that old joke about the kid digging through the pile of horse manure, saying, "I know there's a pony in here somewhere!"

"A lot of these are my fat clothes," Stephanie said.

*Fat clothes? Excuse me?* "Um, we're the same size, Steph. We've always been the same size."

"The same size? Oh, no. No. We are not," she said, with a pitying smile that implied I was completely deluded.

The next bag held shirts, sweaters, skirts, and pants. Okay, this was better. Winter jacket, long wool coat, scarves, gloves, hats. And lo-and-behold, a brand-new pair of boots. Doc Martens. Black. Rugged soles. Trademark yellow stitching. I held them up.

"What's the deal with these? Not your usual style, Sis."

"They're not. Had a wild hair one day and bought them. I don't know what I was thinking. They're too big. I'm not a clunky combat boots kind of gal."

I was glad that I *was* in that moment. I slipped my foot into one of the Docs—not too big, not too small. Just right. I sighed, contented.

The bags emptied, I looked at the heap on the bed. "This is your *extra*? How big is your closet?" She'd moved recently, and I hadn't had a chance to see her new place.

She waved a hand around the Rose Room. "Maybe half the size of this room."

"Geez! Your closet is the size of my apartment bedroom or maybe the whole apartment! Dang! Who needs that much closet space?"

With that "you are so deluded" look again, she said, "I have a *very* high-end job, and I need to dress the part. The people I deal with expect *this*." She waved a hand up and down her body. "This suit alone cost, like, a month's rent. Nobody is going to trust their money to a woman in rags." She pointed at the pile of her cast-offs. "No offense."

"Rags? Stephanie, these are far from rags. There's a whole 'nother neighborhood between these clothes and where *rags* hang out."

She laughed. "I guess you might think that way, living"— she flipped a hand in the air—"here in Three Rivers. But trust me, in The City," she said, articulating each syllable, "things are different. Much, *much* different."

You know how some people stay humble and never forget where they came from? Stephanie is not like that. My sister reminds us on every visit that she may have *lived* here *before*, but she is not—repeat NOT—*from* here now.

I thanked her profusely for her generosity, of course. Gram came in and gushed over the piles, holding a few things up to the mirror to see if maybe they'd be right for her. She took a sweater for herself and a couple of things she thought my mother might want.

Stephanie declined Gram's invitation to stay for dinner, saying she had to get back to The City. "Business, you know, and later, Mason and I have tickets for the theater. And just a heads up—we'll be in Atlanta at his daughter's house for Thanksgiving."

So very busy, so very important is our Stephanie.

As she left, I felt just the tiniest twinge of envy. Twinge? More like a tsunami. I had no hoity-toity career, no rich guy, no Jaguar, no ginormous closet filled with fancy-schmancy clothes. I had nothing much to show for my thirty-five years on earth.

To ease the misery of picturing myself wearing my sister's fat clothes as I drove around in my carful of crickets, I polished off the quart of espresso chip ice cream my mother had stashed in the back of Gram's freezer.

Later that night, I'd just gotten into bed when my cell rang. Vince.

"I heard about the crickets," he said. "Greg should have cleaned the car before he sold it to you."

"Yeah, that would have been nice." I stifled a yawn. "Much as I'd like to chat, I'm in bed already," I said.

"Mmm. I like the sound of that," Vince said.

"Stop! We don't know each other well enough for that."

"For what?" He gave me an innocent tone.

I let go of a yawn. "Did you want something, Vince?"

"Yes, I wanted to say I'm sorry I doubted you about somebody breaking into your place."

"Thanks. Appreciate you saying so. Anything else?"

"You still want to go out sometime?"

"What did you have in mind?"

"How about I surprise you," he said.

I hesitated. "I've had some pretty nasty surprises lately. How about you text me what you're thinking, and then I decide if I want to do it?"

He agreed, and we ended the call. I snuggled under the covers, smiling myself to sleep. Fat clothes, crickets, whatever—my life had just taken a turn for the better.

# CHAPTER FIFTEEN

### Wednesday, November 14

WEDNESDAY MORNING, JUST AFTER nine o'clock, my mother burst into the Rose Room, where Chloe and I were sleeping. "Mackenzie! Wake up!"

I jerked to semi-consciousness, scanning for reasons I needed to be awake. I came up empty. I sat up, rubbing my eyes. "Wuzzup? Why aren't you at work?"

"I'm going in late today, and you have to get up now!" She reached for the covers and grabbed my arm at the same time. Chloe stood and gave my mom a low, throaty growl.

My mother released the bedding and my arm. Chloe laid back down.

"That—" She pointed at Chloe. "That thing hates me. I can tell."

Hmm. I knew cats could be aloof, but could they actually hate someone?

"I doubt that she hates you, Mom. I think she probably just didn't like you disturbing her little nest here in my bed."

"No, she hates me. I walk into a room, and she sticks her tail in the air and walks away."

"Geez, Mom. She's a cat. You make it sound like she's one of the mean girls in school."

"Feels like that. I keep my bedroom door closed at night just in case she decides to attack me in my sleep. She hates me!"

Okay, now that seemed a little paranoid. "But Mom, is it a good idea to close your bedroom door at night? What if Gram needs our help with Nathan? How would we hear her if our doors are closed?"

"If she needs me, Gram can come and get me. Or here's a thought: you keep *your* door closed and keep the cat in here with you."

"Or you could just get to know her and stop thinking a cat hates you. She's a cat, Mom. Just a wee, tiny cat." I ran my hand down Chloe's back. She purred. "See? Sweet and friendly."

My mother moved to pull the covers off me. "You need to get up—" she began. Chloe stood again, arched her back, and hissed.

Mom jumped back. "See that? It's *not* my imagination. That cat is a menace. It's only a matter of time before she tries to claw my face off. She hates me!"

Chloe curled her warm little body next to my side and purred, kneading my arm with her paws. A mini massage from Chloe, the guard cat.

My mother gave a loud grunt of disgust and stomped out of the bedroom.

I hollered after her. "Why did you want me to get up?"

She yelled back, "The police are here to see you!"

# CHAPTER SIXTEEN

I DUG INTO THE PILE of Stephanie's hand-me-downs and slipped into a pair of black sweatpants. Silky smooth against my skin. Not like my usual sweats.

Snarky snarked, *Oh pardon me, it's not sweats . . . it's ath-leeee-zur.* Snarky can be a real snot.

I pulled on Gram's cardinal sweatshirt, ran my fingers through my hair, and headed downstairs barefoot.

I figured the police were following up on the call I'd made to report the robbery at my apartment. Maybe they'd caught the sleaze, and I'd have my stuff back. I smiled, imagining wearing my fave shirt again.

The smile disappeared halfway down the open staircase when I saw who was standing in Gram's foyer. My hand gripped the oak banister, my knuckles going white.

It was her. *Or is it "she"?* Rational Me is a stickler for good grammar.

Standing in the foyer was the female officer who'd worked with my late ex-husband.

*The one Billy cheated on me with.* Snarky didn't care a whit about grammar at that moment. *This is the door the ho is at.*

I took a deep breath, gathering myself as I took the rest of the stairs slowly.

In the foyer, I forced a smile. "Can I help you, Officer?" I said, feigning ignorance. Trying to ignore how good she looked in her uniform, the light blue shirt matching the cornflower blue of her eyes, her blonde hair pulled away from her high cheekbones and peaches-and-cream complexion. Trying not to imagine her with my ex, the sounds they made together.

"Hello, Mackenzie, it's me. Heather Sullivan."

I pretended to think hard. "Do I know you?"

Her cheeks reddened, but her expression said she wasn't buying the act. "Of course, you know me, and I know you." She paused, looked down at her shoes, cleared her throat, and then met my eyes. "I, um, knew Billy."

I stifled the urge to lunge at her and tear out every strand of her perfect hair from her perfect head. Rational Me cautioned, *Perhaps there are better ways to spend the day than under arrest for assaulting an officer of the law. Besides, she's armed.*

I paused for several beats, willing my heart to slow. She waited. Then, my tone as flat and cold as I could make it, I said, "Oh. Yeah. I remember."

"I wonder if you have a few minutes to talk?"

I wasn't about to invite her in. She'd already been "in" enough in my life. "I'm listening." I crossed my arms. She started to cross hers, then let them drop to her sides.

She cleared her throat again. "Okay." She took a breath, blew it out. "I was, uh, sorry to hear about your, um, ex . . . um, Billy."

Angry Me was incensed. *She has no right whatsoever to talk about Billy. None! And she's lucky she didn't try to come to his funeral. She'd have been sorry! I would have bashed—*

Rational Me intervened. *Okay. Okay. Just calm the heck down. Hear her out.*

I tried to focus on my breathing.

Heather continued. "I also wanted to tell you how sorry I am about everything that happened, you know, before."

Angry Me spoke aloud, pushing against the pain of the past and the tears that threatened to spill over. "*Every*thing? That covers a lot, don't you think? And a feeble little apology doesn't quite make up for *every*thing, does it?"

She shook her head, met my eyes. "No, of course not. But I'm in AA now, working with my sponsor, and I wanted to come to say I am sorry for the pain I caused you by my actions. I was stupid. I behaved badly. I take full responsibility for all I did. I hurt you, and I'm sorry. So, so sorry." She held eye contact, waiting.

Ah, Heather was making her amends. I'd never stuck with AA long enough—just that one meeting—to work on the steps, but I'd heard others talk about it. And Billy had left me a note, an apology, as his amends to me.

Heather went on. "Being sober has changed everything for me. I had no idea how many people I'd hurt until I got sober and started my recovery work. I've done so many stupid things!"

I read sincerity on her face as she went on, the words coming faster. "I'm truly—truly—sorry I hurt you. I feel awful about it, and I want you to know that I've changed. A lot. And, well, I just wanted to stop by and tell you that. And I don't expect it, but I hope someday, maybe you'll be able to forgive me."

She let out a huge sigh. "So that's all I came to say. Thanks for listening." She turned to go.

"Heather, wait." Where that came from, I have no clue. Maybe a Kinder, Gentler Me was emerging. She turned to face me. I took a huge breath in and held it for a long moment. With the exhale, I decided.

There had been enough sadness, enough hurt, enough anger, enough pain. It had all gone down years ago. Billy was gone. Maybe it was time for me to move on too. Maybe my recent brushes with death had made me realize that life is, indeed, short. Too short to hold on to anger, pain.

"We can't change the past," I said, "but as my grandmother says, we don't have to let the past ruin the future."

"A wise woman, your grandmother."

I smiled. We could agree on that. Gram was wise, indeed. "Maybe we can try to let the past be in the past."

I offered my hand, and Heather wrapped it in both of hers. It was her turn to tear up. "Thank you. Thank you," she said, pumping my hand. "You have no idea how much I appreciate this." As she let go, Chloe chose that moment to come over to us.

Chloe looked up at me, then at Heather, and then she rubbed against Heather's pant leg. Chloe approved. Who was I to argue?

I smiled, Heather smiled, turned to leave, then turned back toward me. "Oh, one more thing. I heard how you figured out what happened to Billy. Lots of discussion about it at the station. That was some great detective work there."

"Not really," I said. "I just happened to be in the wrong place at the right time, or something like that."

"No, you had the guts to put yourself in that place. Some very impressive badassery going on there. Have you ever thought about being a cop? We could use another female, especially a smart one."

*Twice in one week? First Chief Bronson, now Heather.* I shook my head. "Kind of too late for that, don't you think?"

"Not for our department. There's no upper age limit on recruits. Think about it, okay?" She handed me her official business card. "I wrote my cell on the back in case you ever want to talk. About the police thing, or the past, or whatever."

"Is that part of the whole amends thing?" I couldn't imagine what else we had to talk about as far as the past was concerned. I didn't need details. Billy was dead. Over and done with.

Heather said, "My sponsor encourages me to be completely open to talking things out with the people I've hurt, but only if you want that. I'm just saying I'd be open to talking more in the future, about whatever, if you ever want to. No pressure."

Was she saying we should be friends now? I paused for a moment, waiting to hear Snarky Me trash Heather. But Snarky was silent. Maybe it was Wise Me I heard. *Time to let the past go, to let old hurts be buried with Billy. Let bygones be bygones. Bury the hatchet.*

Wise Me knows a lot of cliches.

Maybe I was ready to get to know this new wiser, kinder, gentler, forgiving part of me, so I nodded. "Okay, yeah, maybe. You never know."

I had another thought and decided to run it past Heather. "Can I ask you something, uh, police-related?"

She smiled. "Sure. What is it?"

"My grandmother is pretty upset about a friend of the family who died this week—Clifford Wilson. She wants me to do some checking just to ease her mind. You know anything about it?"

"Yes, it just so happens I was at the scene," Heather said. (In The City, that would be a huge coincidence. But Three Rivers isn't, as Stephanie reminds us, The City.) "If you want, you can request a copy of the report. There's a form on the department website. The web address is on my card."

I looked down. Yup. There it was.

"Anything you can tell me as a—" I hesitated. Did I want to say it? Yes, I did. "As a friend?" Wow. We'd come a long way in a very short time, but it felt good. Free somehow.

She thought a moment. "Have you ever been to Wilson's house?"

"Not lately," I said. I'd been in the house after Florence's funeral with the rest of the family. And I'd dropped Cliff off there once after I picked him and Nathan up at the senior center but hadn't been inside.

"It's quite the place," she said. "But check out the official report. I can't say anything, really, not even as a friend." She smiled again.

"I can respect that," I said.

She left, and I closed the door, leaning back against it, feeling good about what had just happened. Letting go of the past. Accepting her apology. I felt lighter, like a more noble human being. Generous in heart and spirit.

I picked Chloe up and scratched her head. "Well, that was a surprise, wasn't it, girl? Took guts." I thought about things I'd done to others, especially when I'd had too much to drink. Fights with Billy. Things I'd said in anger. Lies I'd told, excuses I'd made, blame I'd shifted. I wished for a moment that Billy was still alive. Maybe I could offer a few amends of my own to him and to others. Maybe in the someday future, others would be kind to me—if I ever made amends.

But that was for the future, if and when I stopped drinking. Which I didn't plan to do anytime soon because I didn't really have a problem. I could stop anytime I wanted.

I held Chloe at arm's length, hands under her—do cats have armpits? "What do you think about me being a cop? How hilarious is that, huh? Ridiculous, right?" Chloe gave a meow of protest and wriggled. I set her down and walked to the kitchen, thinking.

Wouldn't I need a criminology degree or something, not just a bachelor's in psychology? Besides, Billy had worked there. Too many memories. Too many shadows. No, joining the force wasn't for me, I was sure about that.

But figuring things out, solving mysteries? Chief Bronson seemed to think I had something. Heather had said pretty much the same thing. "Impressive badassery," she'd called it.

Was it smarts? Guts? Instinct? Maybe it was like Gram's intuition, or her *sisu*. I couldn't say for sure exactly what it was, but maybe I did have *something*. And, if I did, what the heck was I supposed to do with it?

# CHAPTER SEVENTEEN

A FTER HEATHER LEFT, I went into the kitchen. Nathan sat at the table, scowling. He'd always had a ready laugh and a great sense of humor, a wink, and a smile for everyone. Kids visiting would go straight to Nathan. He always had gum or candy nearby. Knowing the Nathan of yesterday made it hard to see him as he'd been recently. Angry. Cranky. Short-tempered.

I moved next to Gram as she stirred oatmeal at the stove. "What's up?" I nodded toward Nathan.

Gram shrugged and whispered, "I don't know. He was his old self earlier. Knew who I was. Remembered that Jack is picking him up to go play cribbage this morning." Then louder, she said, "We're having oatmeal. Do you want some too?"

"Sure, Gram, that sounds good." Gram uses the slow-cooking oats and then tops the bowl with brown sugar and whipping cream. "Like having cake for breakfast," she says.

She set a bowl in front of Nathan, who crossed his arms, leaned back in his chair, and snapped at Gram. "I don't want oatmeal!"

"But Nathan, you told me that's what you wanted!" Gram crossed her arms, standing over him, the spoon from the oatmeal pot in her hand, the bowl on the table steaming. Gram was steaming too.

"I never said that! I hate oatmeal. When have I ever liked oatmeal?"

I'd seen him eat it often, heard him say he loved it, but I didn't say that.

Gram took the bowl. "Fine then! Make your own dang breakfast!"

For Gram, this was some serious cursing. She'd said "dang." What was next? Balderdash?

Nathan looked like he wanted to cry. Gram did too.

I spoke up. "Nathan, how about some eggs and toast? I'll be glad to make some for both of you."

"No, you two go ahead! I'm not hungry!" Gram said. Nathan watched her stomp out of the room.

I took his bowl to the sink and asked again, "How about it, Nathan? Eggs and toast?"

Tears brimmed his lower eyelids. "What's wrong with me?" He gave me a pleading look. "What's wrong with me?"

I put a hand on his shoulder. "You're just hungry, I think. Want some eggs?"

"Scrambled?"

I patted his shoulder and smiled at him. "Scrambled it is. Coming right up!" I took eggs from the refrigerator.

"Thanks, Evelyn," he said. Evelyn was his late wife. I wasn't sure how to respond to that, so I said nothing.

After breakfast, Nathan went to the family room to watch television, waiting for his friend Jack to pick him up. Gram—she'd cooled off by then—came back to the kitchen, and we sat at the table with coffee and some of Gram's homemade coffee cake, all warm and melty with butter.

Gram's rooster clock read 10:25 a.m. I told her about Heather.

Gram said, "That was brave, her showing up like that."

"Yeah, bold as brass. Showed up at the front door. I wanted to punch her in the face, but she seemed to be actually sorry for what she did."

"Well, I should hope so! What she did was unforgivable!"

"Maybe, but Billy was the one who couldn't keep it in his pants."

Gram paused. "Are you saying it was *all* his fault?"

"Well, she was at fault too."

"Hmm. Just the two of them?"

Was she trying to say that *I* was at fault? I got huffy, held up a hand. "Hey, I was the innocent victim!"

"Well, Dr. Phil says people don't cheat in a happy marriage."

"Oh, really. Is that proven scientifically?"

"No, but it's proven by my coffee group. We all know that when someone is cheating, it's because something is not right at home. Every time."

I thought about that. Billy'd cheated on me, and Gram's second husband, Chester, had cheated on her. "So, Gram, when Chester—may he rest in peace—was boinking old what's her name—The Hussy—are you saying that was *your* fault?"

Gram hesitated, then said, "Well, no, he certainly made that choice. But I had to admit that we weren't great together. I don't take the responsibility for his cheating, and I think he did have some kind of problem." She cleared her throat. "Ahem. I think he had an addiction." She glanced into the living room, I assumed to be sure that Nathan was engrossed in *The Price Is Right*, then leaned toward me and whispered, "A *sexual* addiction thing. I heard about that on *The View*, or maybe it was *Dr. Phil*."

Her cheeks got pink, and I hid my smile. "So, he had a sexual addiction, and that's why your marriage wasn't great. So, it *was* all his fault."

Gram shrugged. "Well, I wish that were true, but to be honest, I was not the best wife."

"Whatever, Gram. You're one of the most amazing, loving, supportive humans on earth. Chester was too selfish, or addicted, or narcissistic, or whatever to appreciate you."

"And Billy was stupid to do what he did. He should have appreciated how wonderful you are."

That choked me up. Maybe it was the visit from Heather, or the grief, or the sweetness of Gram's presence, but I cried a little, and she patted my hand and let me.

After a bit, I took a breath, blew my nose on a paper napkin, then cleared my throat. "Another thing, Heather said I can get a copy of the police report from Cliff's death. She implied there was something she couldn't tell me because it's against department policy."

"I knew it!" Gram said, smacking a palm on the table. "Something's just not right about the whole thing!"

"Let's not jump to conclusions. I'll get the report, and we'll take it from there. Meanwhile, you probably shouldn't be talking about it with your coffee friends."

Gram promised to keep mum, but I was skeptical. I know how it is when she and "the girls" start yakking.

# CHAPTER EIGHTEEN

HALF AN HOUR LATER, Nathan left with Jack for the senior center, and after Gram and I had cleared away the dishes, she took the Buick to meet her friend Velma and the others for coffee at Hilda's Café on First Avenue, as she does most Mondays.

I should have made her pinky swear not to gossip about anything.

Using my mother's laptop, I filled out the online request for a copy of the police report on Cliff's death, got an email confirming the request was received and that I should allow a couple of hours for it to be prepared.

I put on a short-sleeved blue tee shirt and a gray hooded sweatshirt from Stephanie's athleisure pile. I squeezed myself into a pair of her designer jeans, lying on the bed to get them zipped. Snarky whispered, *Her fat pants? Same size? No way!*

I stood up and checked myself in the full-length mirror on the back of the bedroom door. The jeans made me look skinnier. "Not bad," I said.

*Like a sausage casing,* Snarky said.

Rational Me had a suggestion. *Okay, maybe it's time to cut out the third helpings.*

Snarky added, *And the cookies, candy, cake, pie, chips, ice cream. And maybe drink less wine.*

"Let's not get carried away," I said aloud and headed downstairs.

I decided to kill some time at my best friend Tansy Pemberley's yoga studio while I waited for the email confirmation that the police report was ready. I took Cricket and headed to River Street.

TANSY HAD JUST FINISHED HER YOGA Nooners class and invited me to join her for a little cooldown stretching. As we bent forward into Down Dog, I unbuttoned the jeans at the waist since I wanted to keep breathing. Bent over, I squeezed out my words. "Heather Sullivan came to see me to apologize."

Tansy jerked up to standing, hands on her Lycra-covered hips. "No! She didn't! How dare she show her face? And coming to your gram's place like that?"

I stood, slid the jeans' zipper halfway down. "It's okay, Tans. I think it was really hard for her to come over. But she's in AA now, and this was one of those *making amends* things."

We resumed our yoga flow. Down, up, down. On the upswing, she said, "So she wasn't *really* sorry, just doing that because that's what they make you do in AA?"

"I don't think it's like that. I think you have to be truly sorry. Billy's the one who cheated. She just happened to be one of the girls he did it with." I had no way of knowing how many there had been. I suspected Heather was not the only one.

"Whatever. I don't trust her. She hurt you. You can forgive her, but I'll just keep hating her on your behalf."

We laughed together. Tansy always has my back.

I brought my right foot to my left knee, palms together at "heart center," and then bent deep into Figure Four. I concentrated on the pose because I tend to fall over if I attempt to talk while trying to balance. My version of not being able to walk and chew gum at the same time.

We were both silent for a moment before we straightened up again, and I went on. "Heather gave me her cell number. Told me to call if I ever wanted to talk."

"Seriously. Are you going to?"

"I don't think I need to talk to her about the whole Billy thing. I want to just let all that go. But she said something else."

"What?"

"She said I should think about joining the department," I said, then waited.

Tansy looked thoughtful. "Huh. Being a cop? What do you think about that?"

"I don't know. Seems weird, like Billy's ghost would be following me around. I don't think I'm cut out for actual police work, but—" I paused.

Tansy finished my thought. "But you did feel good figuring out what happened to Billy. And you did get the bad guys. That felt great, didn't it?"

I smiled. "Yeah, it kinda did. And Heather called it impressive badassery."

Tansy laughed. "Badassery! Oh yeah!"

I assumed a bodybuilder pose. "Pumped!" I said with a grunt.

We laughed as I, with no small effort, rebuttoned and zipped up. Then I got serious. "My gram thinks something weird happened to their friend Cliff. I don't see it, but I'm going to do a little digging."

Tansy gave me a level look. "Now, see—that's it, right there. You're 'going to do a little digging.' The rest of us say, 'Okay, well, that's what happened. End of story.' But you always want to dig around, get into stuff. Go beyond what the rest of us would do. Be a cop? I don't know, but I *do* know that whatever you decide to do, you'll be great at it."

And Tansy thinking that I could made me think that maybe I could too.

# CHAPTER NINETEEN

THE EMAIL CAME JUST as I was leaving Tansy's. Cricket chirped all the way to the VISITOR spot in front of the county courthouse at the corner of Lake Street and Cedar. I hesitated at the police department door, hit by a memory of coming here to pick Billy up after a shift. We'd laughed with the other cops, and I'd felt so proud of my husband at the time. Could I work here myself? I was pretty sure the answer to that was no.

Heather saw me come in and brought me the report.

"Wow. That was fast," I said. "I just put in the request a couple hours ago."

She smiled. "Well, we *are* here to protect and *serve*. Let me know if you have questions."

I scanned the report. Heather had been first on the scene and found Cliff on the floor by the fireplace, bleeding from the left temple. Still breathing but unconscious. EMTs arrived right behind her, stabilized Cliff, and transported him to the hospital, where he died without regaining consciousness.

"Pretty straightforward," Heather said.

I'd seen this kind of thing on the Murders and Mysteries channel I watch with Gram. It might have been a *Miss Marple* or maybe an old episode of *Columbo*. The victim falls, hits his head on a glass table, a bookcase, or, like Cliff, the edge of the fireplace bricks, and dies. Or gets smacked with the fireplace poker or a heavy statue and dies. I shared all this with Heather and asked, "Do people really die from that kind of stuff?"

Heather said, "Depends on where they hit when they fall and how hard. And swung full force, something like a fireplace poker, a metal pipe, or a baseball bat can do serious damage."

My hand went to the back of my head where I'd been clunked almost a month ago. I'd seen stars before I blacked out, but it hadn't killed me. I still felt the occasional twinge of pain. Traumatic memory, Dr. Angela might say. Rational Me thought again that I should probably make an appointment to see her.

I glanced down at Heather's duty belt, with all its pockets and pouches for official gear and gizmos. I gestured toward the pouch holding her baton. "That thing could do some serious damage too, right?"

She patted the baton. "Yes, it could. Haven't had to use it. Hope I never do, but I'm glad it's there."

Bashing, stabbing, shooting—all very messy ways to kill somebody. We chatted on about the less messy options: choking, poisoning, smothering, and lethal injection. Such a cheery subject.

I said, "Getting back to Cliff, was there any indication of anything else, other than the fall, that might have killed him?"

Heather looked at the report. "Nope. I'd say the fall did it."

"That's it, cut and dried? Nothing else?"

"Well, there was one thing, but it means nothing." She pointed at a line mid-paragraph. "There. There was a feather in the victim's right nostril. The EMT removed it to start the oxygen."

I looked up at her. "A feather? Weird, don't you think? Where did it come from?"

She shrugged.

"Seriously, Heather. How does a guy end up with a feather up his nose? Was he smothered with a pillow? Is it even possible to kill someone that way?"

She looked around the reception area and, with nobody within earshot, said, "It's possible, but there was no sign of that at the scene."

My parakeets sometimes sent out a blizzard of feathers. "Did he have birds?"

"Nope. No sign of birds or cages. No feathers anywhere."

"What kind of feather was it? Was it little and blue or green or gray, like a parakeet feather? Or big, like a parrot? Or white? A cockatoo feather? Blue jay? Cardinal? Eagle? Turkey?"

"Slow down. It was little, and frankly, I couldn't tell you what color it was. It didn't really look like a feather, but that's what the EMT said it was when he pulled it out. I don't usually look too closely at stuff that comes out of somebody's nose."

"Gross," I said. "What did they do with the feather?"

She glanced at the paperwork. "The report just says it was there. EMT probably just tossed it, I'd guess." She reiterated what she'd seen. "No sign of a bird of any kind in the house. No cages anywhere."

"So, where did the feather come from?"

She leaned forward and lowered her voice. "There's a lot of stuff in that house. I mean, a *lot* of stuff."

"I know Cliff collected Packers memorabilia. My grand-mother told me that," I said.

"Way more than just a Packers collection in there. I can't even describe it. You'd have to see it for yourself."

Was Heather suggesting that I should go to Cliff's house and check around? Anxious Me whispered, *No, she is not suggesting that, and you should definitely* not *do that.*

Rational Me said, *Anxious is right. That's a really dumb idea.*

But Brave Me told them both to hush. Brave Me prefers asking for forgiveness rather than permission. Brave Me was obviously in charge of the Department of—what did Heather call it? Oh yeah. Impressive Badassery.

Anxious Me suggested, *Or maybe it's Impressive Stupidity.* I left my parts to battle it out and returned to the discussion of the police report.

I asked, "No autopsy?"

"No. He died at home, and he'd been under a doctor's care for the dizzy spells. The nephew, what's his name?" Heather glanced down at the report as I supplied the answer.

"Jason is the nephew, and Jillian is the niece."

"Yes," Heather continued. "Jason was there." Jason's statement was part of the report. He'd found Cliff on the floor by the fireplace, unresponsive. His sister had called 911.

I had another thought. "Since he actually died at the hospital, is there a way to look at the medical report?"

"There'd be the death certificate, which is a public record. But his medical records themselves? Only family members or the executor would have access."

"What about the police?"

"We can access records if there's an investigation." I brightened, and she noticed. "But there's no investigation here.

Nothing suspicious. *You* might *think* there is, but *we* have to go on the facts."

"Like the fact he had a feather in his nose? That's not suspicious?"

She snorted a laugh. "Are you kidding? The way that house was hoarded up, I'm surprised he didn't have Brett Favre up his nose!" She saw my expression. "Oops, sorry. That was crude."

"It's okay," I said. I liked the fact that Heather said stuff like that, just blurted out what was on her mind. No wondering what she was thinking. I appreciate that in a person. "I'm going to go over there and ask Jillian or Jason if I can have a look around."

"Why would they let you do that?"

"Maybe I'll take some of Gram's cookies over there, make it a condolence call. While I'm there, I'll look for anything with feathers. And then I'll let you know what I find. How does that sound?"

"I checked the scene, so I don't think you'll find anything. But if you do happen to see anything suspicious—which is highly unlikely—don't disturb it. Take a picture and send it to me. You have my cell, right?"

I had her card with the cell number on the back. I took out my phone and added Heather to my contacts, and she added my number to hers.

She warned me again. "It's very important that you don't touch anything. Touch nothing. Got it?"

I nodded.

"You promise?"

"Scout's honor," I said, raising my right hand, three fingers together. Geez, all we needed now was a pinky swear, but that didn't seem appropriate to do with someone with a gun.

I thanked her, folded the report, and crammed it into the back pocket of the jeans. I left the station, determined to confirm for myself what happened to Cliff. Likely, it was as it appeared: old man fell, died. And the feather meant absolutely nothing.

But Gram had "that feeling." I needed to find out for sure. For Gram's sake and my own.

# CHAPTER TWENTY

NOBODY WAS HOME WHEN I swung by the Victorian. I packed a plastic food container with a dozen of Gram's always-on-hand cookies—six peanut butter and six oatmeal chocolate chip. I hated to give them away because Gram's cookies are heaven-on-earth, melt-in-the-mouth scrumptious. But I thought they might be just the admission ticket I needed to get inside Cliff's house.

And if Jillian or Jason wouldn't invite me in, well, there's more than one way—sorry, Chloe—to skin a cat.

I parked Cricket across the street, down a few houses from Cliff's. His house was on a block of similar homes—all cozy-looking, one- and two-story bungalows, smallish and charming, most in what's called Craftsman style. Well-kept homes, except for Cliff's. His house looked sadly neglected, with overgrown bushes and peeling paint.

I sat with a clear view of the front porch. No lights on in the house, no sign of anyone at home. I checked my phone.

Almost four o'clock. School was out for the day. Jason could be done teaching and on his way home. I had no idea what hours Jillian might be working that day at Lumber City Bank, but my mother was usually home by five.

As I waited, I thought about Jillian and Jason. According to Gram, their aunt Florence felt something was off with them. But like when you play "telephone" as a kid, the story starts as one thing, like "Butterflies are pretty" and ends up something else entirely, like "Butter is bitter." Second-hand or third-hand information is rarely reliable.

I'd met Florence once at Gram's. Nice lady. I'd never met her sister, Jean. Maybe Jean was just a chronic worrier, or one of those mothers who expected her kids to be perfect. She'd died after a fall down her basement steps. No way to check with her.

My opinion of Jillian? Yes, she was odd, but maybe she just had a unique style with that schoolgirl look. Did she honestly wear that get-up every day? She worked with my mother at the bank. Surely, those outfits didn't meet the bank's dress code. I'd have to ask my mother what Jillian was like at work.

Then there was Jason. An imposing figure—well over six feet tall, with his shaved head and always dressed in black. People said Jason was brilliant, maybe even a genius. I wondered why someone of his caliber would want to teach here in Three Rivers.

I knew from Gram and Heather that Cliff's house was full of stuff. Nathan admired Cliff's Packers collection. Maybe ol' Cliff had something in that house that had actual value. Maybe Cliff caught someone trying to steal something, and they killed him. Was that a possibility? I wondered if Jason or Jillian had seen or heard him talking, maybe arguing, with anyone before he died?

"Speak of the devil," I said aloud. Jason stepped out the front door onto the porch to retrieve the mail. I took the cookies and hustled over just as he was heading back inside.

"Jason!" I hollered. He turned. I got to the porch and explained who I was. "Sorry for your loss." I held out the cookies.

He took the container. "Thank you." There was an awkward pause, during which I imagined that he was wondering why some random granddaughter of a random friend of his late uncle's late wife was bringing him cookies. Or maybe he was just waiting for me to speak.

He broke the silence. "Was there something else?"

"I just wanted . . ." I shivered. A north wind had kicked up, and the afternoon had turned chilly. My gray hoodie wasn't quite heavy enough. Jason didn't seem to notice the cold. His short-sleeved black tee shirt stretched over his bulging pecs. The bottom half of the black owl was visible on his massive right bicep. Not exactly the stereotypical ninety-eight-pound-weakling science nerd.

I shivered again and rubbed my hands along my upper arms. "Brr. It's getting cold out here." I glanced with longing toward the open door. Beyond it, I saw stacks of boxes, as if someone was getting ready to move out.

Jason noticed and took a step to the left, blocking my view. "I can't invite you inside."

*Bummer.* "I heard Cliff was quite the collector."

Jason stared at me. "Collector? That's one way of putting it. It's going to take a while to straighten things out."

"I heard he collected Packers stuff."

"Packers, uh-huh. If there's nothing else—" He turned to go into the house.

Clearly, I needed to get to the point. "Wait! I was wondering, did you see or hear Cliff talking with anyone, you know, before he—"

"Before he *what?*" Jason furrowed his brow and gave me a penetrating look.

"Before he fell?" I squeaked the words out.

"Why are you asking?" He loomed over me. I suddenly felt small. Literally and figuratively. I was Dorothy quivering before the great and powerful Wizard of Oz. *Silence, Whippersnapper!*

Anxious Me spoke up. *Yeah, Whippersnapper, why are you asking? This is none of your business. Leave! Now!*

Rational Me took a deep breath. I said, "Well, my grandmother was wondering . . ."

Something—impatience probably—flashed across his face. He frowned. "What's your grandmother got to do with anything?"

"She and Florence were friends, and you know how it is with friends. They, um . . . er, she . . ." I was stammering and couldn't stop myself. I wondered if he could hear how loud my heart was pounding. I crossed my arms, squeezing them against my diaphragm, willing myself to calm.

He stared down at me, expression blank, waiting. Intimidating. I felt like a kid in school trying to explain myself to the principal. Anxious Me fumbled for words. "And she just, that is, we were wondering—" I stopped, swallowed hard.

*Real impressive, Badass,* Snarky said.

I held my breath.

Jason stared at me another moment and then gave me a tight smile that didn't reach his eyes. "Now that you mention it, I did hear the doorbell that day. And I heard Cliff talking with someone."

*Whew!* I exhaled. "Man? Woman?"

"I was playing my music, but I think it was a man's voice."

"Did you hear what they said?"

"Not really. They talked for a while, and then, when I went into the living room, I saw Cliff on the floor. He'd fallen, hit his head on the bricks of the hearth. That's when Jillian came in. She called 911." He reported all this with no emotion. *Just the facts, ma'am.* "I assumed he got dizzy and fell, but now you've got me wondering if someone else was involved. Interesting idea."

"You don't know who the person was or what they wanted?"

"No. Like I said, I was playing my music." Jason paused and looked at the porch ceiling. "Cliff was angry. I did hear him yell something like, 'No way! Never!'" He paused again, thinking. "Yes, yes, that's right. I did hear him say that. Quite upset, angry. Yes, yes, he was."

"Like maybe somebody asking him to do something? Go somewhere? Sell something?"

"Sell, yes, that would be my guess. Could have been the guy next door. The Crandalls have wanted to buy this house. Especially since Cliff stopped taking care of the place. But Cliff insisted the only way he'd leave this place was in a pine box." He paused, looked me in the eye, and said, "He got his wish."

I grimaced at that.

Jason cleared his throat, and his voice shifted into what I assumed was his teacher-in-charge tone. "Thank you for the condolence call. If there's nothing else, I have papers to grade." He didn't wait for an answer. Just turned and went inside. *Class dismissed.*

"Thanks for your time," I said to the closed door.

I got in the car, then realized I hadn't asked Jason about the feather. *Shoot!* He'd dismissed me so abruptly that I didn't want to bug him again. I admit it. The guy was intimidating.

It seemed better to wait until I could look around inside, if I could figure out a way to get in there. Maybe I'd have better luck with Jillian.

I looked at Cliff's house. A woman had died there, and the man who grieved for her had given up. The front gutter had little trees sprouting from it. Woodpecker holes riddled the wood siding. Brickwork along the front of the porch had crumbled away in spots.

Cliff's not wanting to sell the place made sense. He and Florence had built a life in that house. Maybe the neighbor got frustrated that Cliff didn't want to sell, maybe angry enough to fight with him. Or it was possible that someone else wanted something from Cliff's hoard of "treasures," which I really wanted to get a look at.

I decided to ask Cliff's neighbors some questions. Nosy Me got excited. *Ooh, like the cops on TV. Canvass the neighborhood. Ask if anyone saw anything on the day in question. Anyone suspicious lurking about? Any odd noises? And Heather gave us permission, didn't she?*

Anxious Me whispered, *Don't get carried away here. You're not a cop. Mind your own business.*

Gram had made this my business. Her feeling that there might be something weird about Cliff's death was contagious. I needed to do more digging.

One way or another, we needed answers, and Nosy Me knew how to get them.

# CHAPTER TWENTY-ONE

W HEN JASON MENTIONED THE neighbors, he'd gestured to the house next door to his right, which was another Craftsman-style bungalow. Likely built around the same time, but the resemblance to Cliff's house ended there.

This house seemed happy as I approached. The landscaping perfect to the last blade of grass. Bushes neatly trimmed across the front. Pots of yellow and orange chrysanthemums on the front steps formed a welcoming corridor leading to the grapevine wreath adorned with fall leaves and sunflowers on the front door. A row of little smiling wooden scarecrows—joined at the hands and feet like accordion paper dolls—hung across the wreath.

An orange and brown wooden plaque with the words HAPPY HARVEST hung from a hook above the doorbell. Underfoot, a thick mat read:

THE CRANDALLS<br>
WELCOME TO OUR HOME

I rang the bell.

The woman who answered looked about my mother's age. She wore paint-spattered overalls over a tie-dyed shirt, her hair in a gray bun on top of her head. Turquoise paint streaked the side of her nose, and a smudge of magenta graced her left cheek. She wiped more paint from her hands with a rainbow-stained cloth.

"Mrs. Crandall?

She nodded and smiled.

I gave her my name and said, "My grandmother was close to Cliff and Florence. Do you mind if I ask you a few questions? For my grandmother's sake?"

"Of course. Come in. Come in." She swung the door wider, and I stepped inside. She wiped her hands on the cloth, then shoved it into a pocket in her overalls. "Sorry I'm such a mess. I was just in the studio." She gestured toward the back of the house.

"You're an artist," I said, demonstrating my knack for stating the obvious. "What's your medium?"

"Mixed media," she said. "Collage. Assemblage. Whatever strikes me on a given day. Love the feeling of glue and paint on my hands." She wiggled her turquoise and magenta fingers at me.

I laughed. "My friend Jade says the same thing." Jade has been making art since we met in middle school, and she's had several local showings in the last few years.

"Is your friend Jade Kelly?"

"Yes. You know her?'

"Oh yes, certainly. I love her work. Please come into the kitchen. I've got coffee on." I guess any friend of Jade's was a friend of Mrs. Crandall's. I'd have to thank Jade later.

I followed her into a warm red and yellow kitchen that smelled of hazelnut coffee. From the red gingham-checked curtains to the orange-and-yellow-flowered tablecloth, the whole room seemed to smile in welcome.

"Sit, sit," she said. She poured two coffees and removed plastic wrap from a plate of oatmeal raisin cookies. I took one and munched as we sat and talked about how wonderful Jade's art was and which of her works were our favorites from last summer's showing at the local arts center.

After several minutes of Jade-talk, Mrs. Crandall said, "I've forgotten why you said you stopped by."

I explained how close Gram had been to Florence and Cliff. "She needs some reassurance. His death was so unexpected," I said.

Mrs. Crandall nodded. "Yes, we were all shocked. I remember Florence talking about your grandmother. They were great friends, weren't they?" I nodded and she continued. "Everyone got along so well with Florence and Cliff. So difficult for him to lose her. She had cancer, you know. Such a hard time." She looked down at her intertwined fingers. I waited.

After several moments, she went on. "Cliff was always on the quiet side, but Florence was just a delight. She and I talked gardening all the time. You should have seen her dahlias."

Mrs. Crandall looked toward Cliff's house and shook her head. "After she passed, it was never the same around here. Everything just . . . well, I'm sure you're as shocked as we all are about what's happened over there."

"Pretty bad, isn't it?" I played along to keep her talking.

"Oh mercy! Bad doesn't begin to describe it. At first, we thought he just needed time to grieve. But after a year or so, with the weeds growing thicker, we tried to talk with him. We would have mowed and cleaned things up for him but we didn't want to overstep."

A man came to the kitchen doorway. "Who you talkin' to, Bess?"

"Come in, Howard. This is Mackenzie. She's a relative of Cliff's."

I didn't bother to correct her.

Howard Crandall was balding and wore a red and blue plaid shirt and khaki work pants. Suspenders wreathed his substantial paunch. He sat down heavily next to his wife.

"I'm sorry . . ." Howard said, and I assumed he was going for "sorry for your loss," but he continued. ". . . you have to be related to such a miserable—"

His wife laid a restraining hand on his arm. "Be nice, Howard."

He scowled at her. "Ain't got much nice to say." Howard gave me a half smile. "Well, he's gone now, so maybe things will get better."

"May I ask what you mean by that?"

Bess Crandall shot me a look as if to say I'd be sorry I asked. Howard launched into a litany of complaints. "It started right after his wife died. He put up that damn fence."

His wife shook her head. "Now, Howard, you know darn well that fence turned out to be a blessing. It blocked off our view of the mess."

Howard ignored her. "He put up the ugliest solid wooden fence he could find just to spite me. Not just ugly but inside our property line. Cut off a good foot of our backyard! And if that wasn't bad enough, he quit taking care of the place. Have you seen the house, taken a good look? Brickwork's falling to pieces, front porch sagging. Woodpeckers havin' a field day with the siding. Sidewalk's crumbling. These Craftsman homes are masterpieces! How does a man ruin a masterpiece? I don't understand it!"

I shrugged. He went on, his voice louder. "And inside the place! Oh my God! I've seen the mess through the windows. Who keeps every piece of godforsaken crap he finds? Unless he's just crazy. That's all I can think." He slammed a fist on the table.

Bess Crandall raised her voice. "Howard, calm down. You're going to give yourself a stroke!"

Howard took a deep breath, and another, then continued. "We filed complaints about the weeds and not shoveling his walk. Called the city. They issued citations, fines. He ignored 'em all. I offered to buy the place more than once, figured we could fix it up and sell it."

"Like those house flippers on TV," his wife said.

Howard said, "But it don't matter now. He wouldn't sell. Refused to even discuss it! We hoped things would change when those kids moved in."

Bess patted her husband's hand. "You know the kids have tried to make it better. Jason's mowed and shoveled. And they've both tried to take care of the yard, but I can tell neither has a green thumb."

Howard snorted. "The place still looks like a dump. Hurts everyone's property values, but especially ours since we're right next to the mess." He shook his head and repeated, "I just don't understand it. Who lets a Craftsman fall apart like that? Who fills a house with that much crap? He went nuts after his wife died."

Bess smiled at him. "You'd probably do the same if I passed."

Howard shot her a look that indicated he heartily disagreed. She gave his hand a playful slap.

I looked at Howard. "Mr. Crandall, did you happen to go over to see Cliff the day he died?" I wondered if Howard was the man Jason had heard.

Mrs. Crandall shot her husband a cautioning look, shaking her head ever so slightly. "No way! I wouldn't give that—" Howard began. Bess cleared her throat, and Howard softened his tone. "Our last civil conversation was long ago, right after she died. He was still reasonable back then, but there was just no point trying to talk sense anymore." With that, Howard stood up and said, "Nice meetin' you, but I got things to do."

I thanked him, and he left the room.

I stood to leave, then thought of something else to ask Mrs. Crandall. "Do you remember seeing anyone else around the house the day Cliff died?"

She thought a moment, frowned. I waited. She shook her head.

"Well, if you think of anything else—"

She looked in the direction her husband had gone, then lowered her voice. "How can I reach you?"

Nosy Me got excited. *Ooh. She must have secrets to share.*

Rational Me said, *This would be a handy time to have a business card, wouldn't it?* I dug into the purse I'd borrowed from my mother and found a pen and the receipt for Chloe's supplies from Pudasek's Hardware. I wrote my name and cell number on the back of it and gave it to her. She read the receipt side and said, "Oh, you have a cat?"

I told her about Chloe.

"You know, Florence had two cats. After she died, those cats were out and about at all hours. I felt sorry for the poor things, so I'd leave food out for them. They'd bring dead rabbits and mice and leave them on our porch. Howard would get so mad, but they were just bringing us gifts, grateful for the food I left for them. Just because Florence died, that didn't mean her cats should suffer. She was such an animal lover. Had such a generous heart for all living things. Dogs, cats, squirrels. And especially birds."

That got my attention. "She loved birds? Did she have birds in the house?"

"She had a pair of canaries years ago, loved to hear them sing. I could hear them when the windows were open. But they died while she was sick. I asked her why she didn't replace them, and she said she just couldn't bear the thought of losing any more." She gazed out the window, her tone wistful. "Their yard used to be full of birdfeeders and birdhouses. Cliff built a lot of those for her. The cutest little wrens nested in the birdhouse she hung on the clothesline pole in the backyard." She looked at me. "Cardinals were her absolute favorites. She had Cliff plant pine trees to attract the cardinals."

"Did Cliff have birds in the house after she died?"

"Not likely. Birds were Florence's thing. I imagine it would have been too painful for him after she passed. And it's just as well." She nodded toward Cliff's. "How could anything survive in that mess?"

*How indeed? And Cliff didn't.* I asked her to let me know if she thought of anything else, however insignificant it might be.

As we walked to the door, she said, "I'm sorry if Howard was rude." I assured her it was no big deal. She went on. "Florence was such a lovely person. And her dahlias were the envy of the neighborhood. Oh, if you could have seen them!" I left her looking toward Cliff's house, saying to herself, "Such a shame. Just such a shame."

I drove away, wondering if Howard's anger toward Cliff could have become murderous. I couldn't imagine things going that far, but you never know what people will do if they think they've been wronged. Especially when resentment has been building for years.

And Bess Crandall had given me something useful. I still didn't know how a feather ended up in Cliff's nose, but at least I knew there had been birds in the house at some point in the past.

# CHAPTER TWENTY-TWO

Thursday, November 15

I WOKE IN A SWEAT, coming out of a bad dream, willing my heart and my breathing to slow. In the dream, Billy and I were at a cop party in a huge house. He disappeared at some point, and I looked in every room, every space in the place, turning over rocks. I suspected—no, I *knew*—that he was somewhere in the house with another woman. I felt a churning in the pit of my stomach, pressure in my chest, adrenaline fueling a singular purpose: find the jerk and catch him in the act.

Obviously, connecting with Heather had stirred up the past, and the past invaded my dreams.

I'd tracked Billy more than once in real life during our marriage. I'd checked up on him. Why? Trying to confirm for myself that what I sensed was, in fact, true. That his lies about not doing anything were just that—lies, lies, and more lies.

When I'd called him out, told him I knew he wasn't where he said he was, he denied it, and the gaslighting started. *You're overreacting. You're so dramatic. Why would you think that? Can you hear yourself? You're so insecure. You're too emotional. Too sensitive. I never said that. It didn't happen that way. I haven't been* (fill in the blank). *You're imagining things.*

I'd heard it all, and after enough of that, I doubted my own instincts, my own worth, thought I was going crazy. That's what gaslighting does. Dr. Angela had helped me see that.

After I woke up and my heart slowed, I reminded myself of the truth: He was the one who cheated. Billy did that, not me. Whatever my shortcomings, I wasn't the one who chose to cheat. He did. And that ended the marriage.

The truth gave me comfort.

I took a hot shower and put on a long-sleeved tee and a soft-as-a-kitten sweater from Steph's cast-offs. I slipped into a pair of faded jeans my mother didn't wear anymore—they were a little big, but that made me feel thinner. I put on a bit of blush and ran a brush through my hair. I checked the mirror.

Kinder, Gentler Me said, *You're not the least bit fat. Stephanie doesn't know what she's talking about.*

Rational Me piped up. *Still, it wouldn't hurt to cut back on the sweets, just a little. Maybe.*

I've been addicted to sugar for as long as I can remember. I've soothed myself with boxes of Good & Plenty and Mike and Ike. And sometimes when I need extra soothing—feeling sad, angry, or just bored—I wash the candy down with wine.

Dr. Angela had suggested that maybe I had some issues with what she called "addictive self-soothing behaviors." After she said that, I went straight home and hit the Milk Duds, which paired nicely with a chardonnay.

I told Chloe I'd see her later and went downstairs. Gram was waiting in the kitchen, finishing her coffee. I put on my running shoes, took a couple of pieces of toast to eat in the car, and Gram and I headed to Lou's Vintage in the Buick.

When Gram's friend Lou found out I'd been fired last month, she gave me a part-time job working in her store on River Street. Gram wanted to come along to do some shopping on my first day.

Lou's Vintage occupies the first floor of a building that dates to the late 1800s. The building boasts multicolored brickwork arranged in an intricate pattern and a row of four fancy, arched windows on the second floor, topped by a wide arch at the roof line. "Italianate style," Lou tells anyone who asks.

Lou owns the building and lives in the larger of two apartments above the store. She rents out the second unit.

Lou's store is full of treasures, according to Gram. According to me, it's stuffed with stuff. Call it what you want. Bric-a-brac. Tchotchkes. Trinkets. Doodads. Household goods, costume jewelry, old books, and lots of old clothing. Bell bottoms and macrame vests from the 1970s and party dresses from the 1950s and '60s.

"Ooh," Gram said, holding up a black cocktail dress. "You'd look just like Jackie Kennedy in this!"

"Um, Jackie Kennedy? Can't I look like someone from *this* century, Gram?"

Gram frowned. "Honestly, everything is so throw-away now. You kids don't appreciate quality anymore. There's real treasure here."

Lou is in her seventies and is kind of a vintage treasure herself. She's a huge fan of hippie wear, and today, she sported a faded pair of bell-bottom jeans with a KEEP ON TRUCKIN' patch sewn on the butt, topped with a tie-dyed tee under an embroidered denim shirt. A headband tied around her forehead said VIETNAM.

"You look, um . . ." Gram started to say.

Lou said, "Groovy?"

"Okay," Gram said, but her expression said something different.

Lou had spent the last couple of weeks pumping water out of her basement. The Wolf River flooded some of the businesses in the downtown area after the deluge of rain we received at Halloween. Lou had lost several cartons of her treasures, and now, two weeks after the flood, the basement was dry, and Lou was finally ready for me to start "getting all this stuff organized."

I do love to organize stuff. My logical mind loves order and seeing patterns. I always get a little thrill when I notice a digital clock reading 3:33 or 5:55. An even bigger thrill if I happen to catch the time at 2:22 on February 22.

I like patterns and order and solving logic problems. I like challenges. When I have a goal, I persist until I get it done. That rational, goal-directed, persistent part of me was delighted when Lou pointed at a huge pile of boxes in her main floor storeroom. "There. Those boxes. See what you can do with them."

People donate things to Lou all the time. But she also travels to hit the sales. Estate sales. Garage sales. Yard sales. Tag sales. Whatever you call them in your neighborhood. One person's trash will be, Lou hopes, someone else's treasure.

"I'm like a matchmaker," she says. "Matching people with stuff." And given that she does a steady business, people appreciate what she does.

Gram let me know she was leaving and told me to call the house when I was ready to go home. I gave her a hug, and she left in the Buick.

I sat on a wooden chair in Lou's back room, bent over, and opened the first box. Clothing. I set it aside. Next box. More clothing. Third box. Books.

I hollered to Lou. "What kind of books do we sell?" Already it was "we," as if I were taking ownership.

She came to the doorway. "Keep the old hardcovers with sewn bindings." I knew those were popular with local artists, like Jade, who created altered books with the old ones. "The newer books have glued bindings. Unless it has an interesting title, those can go into the dump. We sell a lot of mystery novels and anything that's got a hunky guy with flowing hair on the cover." Ah, yes, romance novels. Always a market for those.

I sorted through the box of books. A couple of Sue Grafton's alphabet mysteries. *T Is for Trespass.* I hadn't—not lately, anyway. *V Is for Vengeance.* None of that lately either—thank goodness. I put them in the keep pile.

The rest of the books—non-romance, non-mystery, non-sewn—I put back in the box and set it by Lou's back door for the trash bin.

I opened the last box and felt my heart jump into my throat. My flannel PJs with the cute teddy bears dancing, old and faded but oh-so-comfy, right on top. I dug in. My sweaters, my underwear, my socks. Kyle's blue sweatshirt. He'd be thrilled.

"Lou! Where did this box come from?"

She came back to the doorway. "Which box?"

"This one! It's full of my stuff!" I explained how Vince and I had discovered someone had taken my clothes and emptied my jewelry box.

I pawed through, shaking things out, hoping to find the family brooch. No jewelry and no sign of my favorite shirt. I wanted to swear, and I wanted to cry.

Lou crouched to take a closer look. "This box was at my back door when I opened up yesterday morning. People do that, leave donations back there."

I held up the teddy bear pajama pants. "Smell these! Smoke! This is *my* stuff, and whoever left this is the thief who ripped me off!" Anger trumped tears.

Lou said, "Maybe the police could get fingerprints off the box?"

"Who knows how many people have handled this? And what will the cops say? 'Big deal. Somebody took stuff from a burned-out building and dumped it here.' Not exactly grand theft."

Snarky added her two cents. *What do you know about grand theft or felonies or petty theft or burglary? Geez, you're a dope. Don't bug the cops with this. They have enough to handle, not that this town has a lot of crime, but still.*

Lou interrupted my thoughts. "Should we call the police?"

"I don't know if there's a real crime here. Just some low-life looking for stuff to hock, maybe." Vince was probably right about that. "Anyway, at least I have some of my stuff back, even if my favorite shirt and the brooch aren't here." I described the waves of rhinestones.

"Oh, sure, I remember that brooch," Lou said. "Your grandma had it and then gave it to your mother, right? And then it came to you? I'll keep my eye out. You never know. It might show up here. But I think we should at least make a report to the police. I don't want to get into trouble down the road for receiving stolen property."

I hadn't thought of that, but she was probably right. Lou made the call.

An hour later, one of Three Rivers' finest—a young cop named Burns with a buzz cut and muscles for days—came to the store. He scribbled notes on a little notepad as I told him my story, describing my favorite shirt in detail.

Officer Burns gave me a look. "A shirt. Seriously?"

I got a little defensive. "Well, it was my favorite shirt! And I want it back!"

He made more notes as I described the brooch. "What's the value of the jewelry?"

I wished I could say a million dollars, but the truth was it was just a fake. "It's got sentimental value," I said.

"Like the shirt."

"Yeah, okay. No monetary value. But don't *you* have things that have value to you even though you can't put a price tag on them?"

He shrugged. "We're not talking about me here. Is there anything else you need to report?"

He waited. For the life of me, I was having trouble picturing my apartment as it had been before the fire. How quickly we forget.

"No, I guess not. Just the shirt and the brooch," I said. "Oh, wait. I had maybe fifty bucks in cash in the kitchen. That's gone too."

*Now* that's *petty,* Snarky whispered.

Officer Burns raised his eyebrows, no doubt agreeing with Snarky. He took several pictures of the box with his phone and handed me his card. He said I shouldn't hesitate to call him if I thought of anything else, but I don't believe for a hot second that he really meant that.

After he left, Lou said, "Nothing more we can do today." She was ready to close the store.

I told her I'd be back the next day and called Gram to pick me up.

Lou said, "We can do every other day if that's better for your schedule."

"I have no schedule at the moment. I'm totally flexible." *Nothing going on. At a dead end. Starting over from scratch. Ripped off. Burned out. Ugh.* I heaved a sigh.

Lou patted my arm. "Things will work out, Mackenzie. I'm sure of it. And since you're flexible right now, let's plan on you being here every day until things are organized. Then we can decide what will work longer term. How does that sound?"

I agreed. Going to Lou's every day would get me out of the house and give me something to do and to focus on besides my past, my present, and my future.

All of which felt pretty sucky at that moment.

# CHAPTER TWENTY-THREE

### Friday, November 16

I DROVE CRICKET TO LOU'S Friday morning—my "passengers" chirping all the way. I spent a couple of hours making little headway with the organizing project. Around noon, Lou hung a "Closed for Inventory" sign on the front door and said she was going out of town to an estate sale, and we could knock off for the weekend. I had no problem with that.

Nosy Me had an agenda.

Heather Sullivan hadn't seen any sign of birds in Cliff's house. But Mrs. Crandall had said that Florence did indeed have canaries at some point in the past. I called my mother at Lumber City Bank.

"Is Jillian working today?" I asked.

"I can see her from my desk. She's at her teller's window. Why?"

"Just text me if she leaves the bank, okay?"

I heard the tension in my mom's voice. "Why? What are you doing? I hope you're not doing anything stupid."

Snarky Me wanted to say, *No, Mommy, I'm not going to burn myself with hot syrup, and yes, Mommy, I washed my hands.* But Kinder, Gentler Me knew she was just anxious, so I assured her I was not doing anything stupid. I don't think she believed me.

I wasn't sure if I believed me either.

Jillian was at work, and since school was in session, I was pretty sure Jason would be in class all day.

Nosy Me decided it was a perfect time to go to Cliff's house again and maybe get a look inside. Nosy didn't care what that involved. If I could get inside, I'd check the main floor, upstairs, and the basement. Birds? Feathers? There had to be something somewhere.

I knocked on Cliff's front door, listening. No sounds from inside. I pulled my hand into my sweater sleeve before I touched the doorknob. Anxious Me thought this was a good way to avoid leaving fingerprints.

Anxious Me uses this same technique when leaving a public restroom to avoid picking up nasty germs from the door handle just in case the person before her wasn't as anxious about germs as she is. (Dr. Angela had suggested that I might have a touch of OCD when I told her that. A box of Hot Tamales and half a bottle of Merlot later, I was sure Dr. Angela was imagining things.)

I turned the front doorknob. Locked.

I walked around the house to the backyard. Cliff had a small patio back there with a rusting metal table and four chairs covered in a thick layer of dust and pollen. An old barbecue grill sat at the edge of the patio, a huge spiderweb lacing the underside. A grill could be a place to burn things, say a feather pillow that had been used to smother somebody.

Checking to be sure nobody was home in the web, I opened

the grill lid. No sign of recent use, just the charred remains of some kind of meat and a pile of charcoal dust. No feathers.

I took the skinny sidewalk to the garage on the alley, stood on tiptoe, and peeked in. The single stall was empty. I wondered who got to park in the garage. Jillian or Jason?

Cliff had stopped driving when he started having his dizzy spells. Jillian was driving Cliff's gray Ford Taurus. I'd seen it when she dropped Cliff at Gram's.

Jason, taking his Man in Black theme to the nth degree, drove a shiny black truck with a black interior. "Fully tricked out," as brother Greg described it, a note of envy in his voice.

Behind the garage was a green trash receptacle, the white TREE logo on its side. TREE stands for Three Rivers Environmental Engineering. A fancier name than Garbage R Us.

I'd seen snoopy detective types on TV digging into trash cans and even diving into dumpsters. I lifted the lid and felt a wave of relief that it was empty. If someone had used a feather pillow to smother Cliff and then thrown it away, it was long gone. And I wasn't about to go traipsing through the landfill, no matter how much Gram and Nosy might want me to.

As I closed the trash can lid, I heard the hydraulic grinding of a garbage truck and looked down the alley. A green TREE truck was at the last house on the block. I ran toward it.

The driver was ready to get back into the cab.

"Excuse me!" I hollered over the truck noise. He stopped and turned.

"Did you notice any pillows in the trash can back there?" I yelled, gesturing toward Cliff's.

He scowled at me and shouted. "Pillows? Are you serious, lady? Hell no! I *collect* the garbage. I *haul* the garbage. I *dump* the garbage. I don't *look* at the garbage!"

"Fine!" I shouted back. "I get it! You don't *look!*"

He gave me the finger, got in the cab, and the truck rumbled away. I stomped back down the alley, vowing to never use TREE as my trash hauler if I had a choice in the future.

I'd cooled off by the time I knocked on Cliff's back door. Knocked louder. No answer.

I pulled my hand up into my sleeve again and tried the back doorknob. It turned. I leaned forward. The door opened.

Okay, so this was one of those moments. I held my breath. My stomach knotted. My heart skipped a beat.

I heard Anxious Me. *What the hell are you doing? T Is for Trespass, remember?*

There are real-life detectives—professionals—whose job it is to figure stuff out, solve crimes, unravel mysteries. And then there are people like me. Average citizens—accidental detectives—who get caught up in figuring stuff out. Why? Maybe we just have logical minds. Maybe we can't let go of something once we latch onto it. Is that an OCD thing? Maybe we're stubborn. Maybe just nosy.

In my case, all of the above. Quite the combination.

Besides a love for puzzles and patterns, I love math, too, because there's always a right answer. Things are black and white in math world. No fuzzy gray maybes. Two plus two equals four. Every. Time.

I stood at the threshold of Cliff's back door, curious. Okay, nosy. I stood there, knowing I was going to step forward into law-breaking territory. Why? Because something didn't add up. I needed to know how the feather ended up in Cliff's nose.

I took a step through the doorway. Anxious Me warned, *Stop! Get out! Trespassing. Breaking and entering!*

Nosy Me answered, *No, it is not. The door was open.*

I called out, loud enough for neighbors to hear, "Anyone home? Your door was open! I'm coming in!"

I stepped into the kitchen. I called again. "Hello? Anyone here?" Silence.

The kitchen seemed in order, a normal-looking space, but when I stepped through the swinging door into the dining room, my breath caught in my throat.

# CHAPTER TWENTY-FOUR

BOXES AND BOXES—HUNDREDS OF them—filled Cliff's dining room. Cardboard boxes and plastic bins were stacked around the room, in some spots taller than I am, with a narrow path winding through them. The stack on half of the dining room table brushed the chandelier, with more boxes parked under the table.

The other half of the table was piled high with Green Bay Packers football stuff. Jerseys folded in a stack. Cups, plates, and beer steins emblazoned with green and gold. Pennants and playing cards. A couple of helmets. Plaques and pictures, books and bobbleheads.

In the corner of the dining room next to the windows facing the Crandalls' house, Brett Favre stood. A life-size cardboard cutout. Creepy. Watching me.

I took my cell from my pocket and started snapping pictures. I figured I could look at the pictures later, maybe see something I'd overlooked in the moment.

*Ooh, ooh, just like the cops examining photos from the crime scene. You're like a* real *detective here.* I told Snarky to give it a rest.

I wound my way along the path through the dining room labyrinth, past stacks and stacks of old magazines shoved in between the boxes. My nose itched from the years of dust.

I paused at the fireplace in the living room, picturing Cliff on that floor. *This is where he fell.* I suddenly felt I was intruding.

I turned toward the living room.

I'd seen enough TV programs about hoarding to know that this absolutely qualified. I did a quick survey of the living room, saw what looked like several old stereo cabinets, and, in the corner, a stack of old record players—the kind that comes in a little suitcase. Piles of vinyl records and old 45s like my mother had back in the day. And more boxes in every available inch of space.

Curious, I opened one box. Costume jewelry. I felt another pang thinking of my missing brooch. The next box, more jewelry. Another held a set of plates with different birds on each plate and cup. More boxes of pink, blue, and green glassware. I'd heard the term "depression glass." Seemed appropriate. This whole place was depressing.

As curious as I was about what was in all the boxes, I reminded myself of my true mission here: figure out how Cliff got a feather up his nose. Look for a birdcage. No sign of one in the living room or the dining room. None in the kitchen or bathroom.

I followed the path from the dining room to the main floor bedroom I guessed had been Cliff's.

I flicked on the ceiling light. A double bed, rumpled covers, against the far wall. Two dressers in the room, one holding a television, the other's top obscured by a pile of clothing, with more clothes on the floor. And around the room more boxes, several with AS SEEN ON TV.

The magic dusting cloths. The magic mops. The magic stain removers. All, no doubt, left unused. Maybe Cliff had wanted to do something about the mess in his house. But of course, thinking about it, buying the supplies for it, and talking about it doesn't get the job done.

Rational Me knows. *Only actually clearing clutter will clear the clutter.* I'd learned that from my mother, who learned it from Gram. I come from generations of clutter-clearing women.

I walked around taking pictures of Cliff's bedroom but found no birdcage, no evidence of birds of any kind. The door to the single closet stood open. I poked my head inside. Women's clothing—no doubt, Florence's. A strong scent of perfume, probably her Chanel. But no birdcage.

Off the dining room, a stairway led to the second floor, where I assumed Jillian and Jason had their bedrooms. I called up the stairs just in case someone was up there napping. "Anyone there?" Into the silence, I called, "I'm coming up!"

# CHAPTER TWENTY-FIVE

I WAS ABSOLUTELY GOB-SMACKED BY the difference upstairs from the mess downstairs. Two bedrooms with a bathroom between them. The first bedroom in crisp white and beige. I peeked in the closet. Plaid skirts and white blouses on one end, business wear on the other. Jillian. Her bedside table held only a small, framed photograph of a red-haired woman and a girl, maybe age ten or so. The woman smiled into the camera. The girl, a mini version of her, looked solemn, sad. Jillian and her mother, I assumed.

The other bedroom was obviously Jason's—everything in shades of gray with black accents.

I took pictures. These two were certainly consistent. In each of their rooms, the bedspreads were wrinkle-free, edges level with the floor. Pillows smooth and precisely placed. I could never make my bed that perfectly.

No clutter anywhere. No dust. Nothing out of place. No magazines. No dishes from late-night snacks. Just clean. Pristine.

I like clean and pristine, but this felt sanitized.

In the bathroom, a ceramic toothbrush holder attached to the tile over the sink held two identical toothbrushes, one with a black handle, the other white. Not hard to guess which was whose.

I opened the medicine cabinet above the sink with my sleeve-covered index finger. The bottom shelf held only a half-used tube of Crest neatly rolled up from the bottom around a plastic key. On the middle shelf, women's Secret deodorant, a little bottle of Scope, and a tiny bottle of Chanel No. 5. The top shelf held a razor, shaving cream, Old Spice Swagger deodorant, and aftershave. Normal stuff.

Rational Me liked the idea of being so clean, so organized, so minimalist. Everything in its place.

But Anxious Me thought it weird that there was no sign of a drip, a drop, or a drizzle on any of the containers—as if someone had taken care to wipe them clean. And they were arranged neatly.

Too neatly, as if somebody had used a ruler to line things up. Who? Jillian? Jason? Both? Was this uber-neatness a natural reaction to the clutter in the rest of the house? I could imagine myself wanting to create a little oasis of clean and calm space if I'd lived with Cliff.

Anxious Me wasn't buying that. *Nope. This is way too neat. Hyper-clean. Gotta be some serious obsessive-compulsive stuff going on here. I don't like it! Get out!*

I closed the cabinet with my elbow and was heading for the stairs when I heard sounds coming from the dining room. A man's voice carried up the stairwell. "Son of a b—!"

I froze, panic rising. He swore again. His voice didn't seem as deep as Jason's. I hoped to God I was right about that. Whoever it was, he was moving things around, taking the Lord's name in vain and dropping F-bombs left and right. Gram would have threatened to wash his mouth out with soap.

Rational Me urged, *Look around for something—anything—to use as a weapon!*

Anxious Me just kept whispering, *Ohmigod, ohmigod, ohmigod . . .*

Weapons? Nothing. Couldn't hurt anyone with a tube of Crest. I tippy-toed back to Jillian's room, hoping I wouldn't step on a creaky floorboard. I opened her closet. A plaid skirt wasn't going to help much. I looked down, hoping for a saddle shoe.

*Well, well, well, what is this?* Tucked in the corner of the closet, Jillian had a pair of high heels. Stilettos. Bright red. *Jillian? Miss Plaid Skirt and White Knee Highs? You little vixen!* Snarky was impressed.

I grabbed a stiletto, holding it above my head, and stood to the side of the bedroom door, just in case whoever-it-was came upstairs.

I waited an eternity, holding my breath, ready to defend myself.

Cussing continued, and then things got quiet downstairs. Had he left? I crept toward the stairs. Just as I reached the top of the stairwell, I stepped on a floorboard that creaked loudly.

I heard a clunk from the dining room, then the sound of footsteps running toward the kitchen.

I waited. Heart pounding in my ears, I heard nothing but the sound of my own breathing. I crept down the stairs, right hand gripping the red stiletto, pointy heel end out. At skull height. Just in case.

I paused mid-staircase. Listened. Nothing.

I reached the dining room. Nobody. The swinging door into the kitchen had just stopped moving. I pushed it open with my left shoulder, stiletto at the ready. Nobody in the kitchen.

The back door stood open. I crossed to it and looked out. Nobody in the yard.

Whoever it was, he was long gone. I hoped.

I pushed the back door closed with my elbow. I considered calling Heather to report the guy, but what would I say? *Hey, Heather, a guy broke into Cliff's house. How do I know? Well, you see . . .* Yeah. No easy way to explain this.

I went back to the dining room. "Hey, Brett," I whispered. He wasn't as creepy as he seemed at first. Nice to have backup.

*You're thinking like a crazy person*, Anxious Me warned. *And you're still holding Jillian's shoe.* Anxious had a point. It wouldn't do to leave the stiletto lying around. I ran upstairs, used my shirt to wipe my fingerprints off the shoe, and put it back where I'd found it. I trotted back down the stairs.

After the ultra-clean of the upstairs, the main floor clutter felt oddly comforting. I wondered how Cliff felt here. I'd heard that hoarders find comfort in their possessions, that sometimes when you've lost something precious, you hold on to other stuff. Maybe that's what happened to Cliff after Florence died. Maybe this mountain of stuff offered him permanence somehow. It all had an immovable quality.

I looked around, wondering what the guy I'd heard had been doing. Hard to tell with all the stuff, but it seemed to me that the pile of Packers stuff had been rearranged. I tried to remember what had been there before. Like those puzzles where you compare two pictures and try to identify the differences between them. "What's different here, Brett?"

He didn't have a clue, and neither did I.

I was ready to get the heck out of Dodge when I heard a noise in the boxes. I froze. Mouse? I shivered, recalling recent rodent encounters. Heard it again. Sounded bigger than a mouse.

I was ready to bolt when out from behind a stack of boxes it came. Scrawny, fur missing in patches across its body. One of Florence's cats, maybe. Mrs. Crandall had said there were two.

"Oh, kitty! Poor, poor kitty! Where's your buddy?" It looked at me quizzically. It opened its mouth, but no sound came out.

I swallowed hard against the lump in my throat and shook my head. "Sorry baby, I can't help you right now." It disappeared back into the stacks.

I didn't want to look for cat food in the kitchen or feed the poor thing. I'd promised Heather I wouldn't touch anything. I promised myself I'd make an anonymous call to animal control after I got done with my search.

I looked around for a second cat, moving boxes to peer behind the stacks. "Here, kitty, kitty. Where are you?"

I moved a box. A stench rose. I gagged. Something—I didn't want to know what—was dead in the box. Or under it.

My stomach turned, and I gagged again. I shoved the box back in place and, as fast as I could move through the maze, I headed for the front door and fresh air. I pulled the front door shut behind me, and on the porch, I bent over, taking in big gulps of air, eyes closed, trying to block out the images of what might have caused that smell.

*Dead things. Ugh.*

# CHAPTER TWENTY-SIX

**B**REATHE IN, BREATHE OUT. I hunched, doubled over on the porch, squeezing my eyes shut against the vision of that poor, starved kitty and wishing I could un-smell whatever that was in the house.

I opened my eyes, looking down at two black-and-white saddle shoes. I looked up at Jillian. She was in dress slacks and a sweater. Not a plaid or a knee-high in sight.

"Mackenzie? What are you doing here?"

I thought, or rather lied, fast. "Just came by to talk to you, actually," I said. "Don't know what happened, but I got a little dizzy while I waited."

She eyed me. "You waited out here?" She glanced toward the door.

*Think fast!*

I lied. "Yup. Just got here a few minutes ago. I knocked and rang but nobody answered."

She seemed to buy that. "I'd invite you in, but the place needs a good cleaning."

Snarky snarked, *Understatement of the century.*

"Let's sit out here," she said, and we sat on the top step. "What did you want to talk to me about?"

*Think faster!* "Well, my grandmother . . ."

Jillian smiled. "Your grandma is so sweet. Those cookies she sent over were delicious. Uncle Cliff and Aunt Florence had such good times with your grandmother and Nathan. How is he doing, by the way?"

Nice of her to remember seeing us at the hospital. "He's okay. It was just a temporary thing. He's fine now."

"You must be so relieved." She paused, waited.

"So, my grandmother was wondering, um, that is . . ." I fumbled for an opening as Snarky whispered, *Ooh. Smooth. Some detective you are.* I took a breath and plunged on, asking a question I already had an answer for. "Where exactly was Cliff when he fell?"

She leveled a look at me. "Why do you ask?"

"Well, my grandmother asked me to ask—"

She paused, considering, then said, "Inside by the fireplace. He has a little problem with clutter."

*Little? Ha!* Snarky held back a snort.

Jillian continued. "There's just a little path by the fireplace. That's where he was. It was tough for the paramedics to get to him with their equipment."

"Poor Cliff. What do you think happened?"

She eyed me again for a long moment, then shrugged and looked down at her saddle shoes. "How should I know? I'm not a doctor."

"But you are a family caregiver, like my grandmother. She knows everything about Nathan, what he's like day by day. She knows him better than the doctors know him. So, what do you *think* caused Cliff to fall? Just your opinion."

She shrugged again, looking out at the street. "He'd been having dizzy spells, so I assume it was one of those."

Everyone assumed that, and I would have too. Except for the feather in his nose. That was the only thing.

I shifted gears, testing the waters. "What if he *didn't* get dizzy and fall? Is there anyone you can think of who might have wanted to hurt Cliff?"

Her eyebrows shot up. "Hurt him? I can't imagine any-one—" She stopped, glancing at the neighbor's house. "That Mr. Crandall next door didn't get along with Uncle Cliff, but I can't imagine he'd hurt him." She thought a moment. "But, you know, there was a guy here a week or so ago. Very adamant about buying back some football helmet. I overheard him say that his wife sold it at a garage sale while he was out of town. It looked perfectly ordinary to me, but who knows what some-thing might be worth. The guy was so mad. He and Uncle Cliff yelled at each other."

Ah. I'd seen a couple of helmets in the pile of Packers stuff on the dining room table. Was one missing now? *Some eyewit-ness you are, Brett.*

Jillian continued. "I think the helmet probably came with this Brett Favre thing. I don't care what kind of superstar quar-terback he was. It's creepy." She shivered.

I kept my expression blank. "Who? Brett Favre? What?"

"Yeah, it's one of those big-as-life cardboard cutouts, like they use in stores to get your attention. Gives me the creeps, like one of those paintings where the eyes follow you when you walk by." She shivered again.

"Sounds hideous," I said, but thought, *Sorry Brett. You're not so bad.*

"I'll be glad to see it gone with everything else when we sell the house."

I had wondered what the plan was. "So, you'll be selling? You're Cliff's only relatives, aren't you?"

"There's just Aunt Florence's cousin Sadie in New Jersey. Nobody else. Uncle Cliff said the house would be ours when he added Jason and me to his bank accounts. It just makes things much simpler."

Snarky Me offered up a theory. *Much simpler, indeed. Work at the bank, finagle your way onto all the accounts, and then bump off the old guy. Real nice.*

Rational Me countered that. *Or maybe be compassionate family caregivers and inherit things legitimately.*

"Where will you live after you sell?"

Jillian brightened. "I want to move to a city—New York or San Francisco. I'm tired of this little town." Huh. She sounded like big sister Stephanie. Ambition. Big plans.

"What about Jason? What's he going to do? He's been teaching at the high school how long now?"

"Forever, it seems. He'll travel, probably see the world. Maybe go back to Brazil. That's where he did his semester abroad in college. He's got options. He's a genius."

"So I've heard," I said, steering us back to the matter at hand. "Other than the neighbor and the guy wanting to buy the helmet, nobody else has really been around?"

Jillian shook her head. "No. Nobody that I'm aware of."

"Did the guy who wanted the helmet leave his name and number?"

"I'm not sure. Why?"

I lied. Again. "Nathan's a big Packers fan. Maybe the guy has other things he'd like to sell."

Jillian nodded. "Okay, I'll look around and let you know."

The truth was I wanted to track the guy down, and if I recognized his voice, I could let Heather know, somehow, that he'd broken into the house and maybe even had something to do with Cliff's death.

Anxious piped up. *Somehow, without implicating yourself!*

Snarky replied. *Well, duh, we're not stupid!*

Rational Me weighed in. *First things first. Find the guy.*

Jillian and I exchanged cell numbers. I thanked her for her time, and then, halfway down the front steps, I turned around. "Jillian? One more thing."

Snarky was impressed. *Ooh, just like Columbo.*

Jillian turned, her hand on the front doorknob.

I asked, "Did Cliff have any pets?"

She hesitated. "No. Why?"

"Just curious. I have a couple of parakeets. Do you know if he ever had parakeets?"

She frowned. "No, but canaries—" She stopped, looked at the porch ceiling. I waited. After several moments, she shook her head, looked at me, and said, "But Aunt Florence had those years ago. Why?"

"Did you think of something else?"

She shook her head. "No. No, nothing. Just remembering Aunt Florence's canaries."

I thanked her again for her time and was at the bottom of the steps when she spoke. "You know, it couldn't be helped, right?"

I stopped, took a deep breath, and turned to look up at her. "What do you mean?"

"I mean, he had a stroke or something. And that's why he got so dizzy. We did the best we could, but some things you just can't help. Right?"

"Of course. Everyone knows you and Jason did the best you could."

She thanked me and went into the house. I walked away thinking. Had they done their best? Or had one of them decided it was time for ol' Cliff to shuffle off this mortal plane and helped the process? Or had someone else? Maybe other neighbors had seen or heard something. Maybe this guy who wanted the helmet lived nearby.

Note from Rational Me: *Continue to canvass neighborhood just like they do on TV.*

Note from Snarky: *Wow. You're some kinda genius, Sherlock.*

Note from Kinder, Gentler Me: *Play nice, girls.*

# CHAPTER TWENTY-SEVEN

I T WASN'T UNTIL I was back at Gram's that I remembered I'd silenced my cell phone when I got to Cliff's house. I was ready to yell at my mother for not warning me that Jillian was on her way home. Then I saw that she had texted at 3:30:

> Jillian just left

Maybe I should have told her to send that text in code. Something like:

> Package on its way

But that might have raised my mom's suspicions that I was, indeed, doing "something stupid."

How did real detectives manage to get important messages while undercover without giving away their location?

Nosy was thrilled at the thought. *Ooh, were we just* undercover? *Did we just pull off a* clandestine *operation?*

Maybe I *was* a detective at heart. Maybe I should be a cop. Maybe I could be a spy. Maybe I could work for the CIA.

Maybe I was getting carried away.

I'd done a good job of pretending I hadn't been inside the house. I'd lied straight to Jillian's face without a single qualm. Another minute inside, and Jillian would have caught me. With that thought, I felt something. Not guilt. Not shame. Instead, I felt a kind of buzz, a little thrill at the thought of almost getting caught.

What was happening to me? I'd never been the kid who skipped class or told lies for the fun of getting away with things. I was a rule follower. I colored inside the lines.

Then what was this little kick I got from breaking the rules?

I stopped in Gram's powder room to wash my hands for dinner. Lather, rinse, repeat. Repeat. My hands felt nasty after being in the hoard, almost touching that dead whatever-it-was.

The girl in the mirror had no business breaking into Cliff's house. No business snooping around, asking questions, looking in garbage cans and barbecue grills. No business digging through someone else's stuff.

I'd had no business breaking into that cabin last month after Billy died.

Rational Me remembered: *Yes, Anxious, you were right. We were trespassing.*

Anxious Me: *Told you so! And we were trespassing again today!*

Drying my hands, I reminded my reflection that I'd trespassed and almost gotten caught in Cliff's house. That I'd been ready to bash some guy with a stiletto.

"Seriously? Who *are* you?" I said aloud.

The girl in the mirror couldn't stop grinning. She winked. *I'm an impressive badass. Remember?*

"Yeah, okay. Whatever." I folded the hand towel, hung it on the towel bar, evened up the edges, smoothed the wrinkles out of it, and flicked off the light.

I went into the dining room. My brother Greg and his family were at the table with Gram and Nathan. On the menu tonight: meat loaf, mashed potatoes with butter, green beans, and baking powder biscuits. I can't imagine food more comforting than Gram's.

I sat next to Nathan. The family chatter faded to the background as I ate and thought.

Cliff did indeed have more than a "little clutter problem." And there was someone—maybe two someones—who wanted something from him. The guy who wanted that football helmet. Had he come back to take it, gotten violent earlier, maybe causing an old man's death?

And the neighbors who wanted to buy his house. Howard Crandall obviously was not a fan of Cliff's, but was he angry enough to hurt him?

Lots of questions, and few facts: Cliff fell by the fireplace, hit his head, and died. Maybe it was just what it looked like.

Except for that danged feather. Something else niggled at the back of my brain. What was it?

Snarky spoke up. *You don't have much else up there, Sherlock, so you should be able to figure out what's bugging you.*

Kinder, Gentler Me whispered, *Just relax. Whatever it is will bubble to the surface. Have some more meat loaf.*

I looked at the platter on the table. One thick slab of Gram's meat loaf remained. "Anyone want that?" I asked, gesturing with my fork. No one else claimed it, so I reached, stabbed it, and thunked it onto my plate. In a fancier family, the polite thing might have been to say, "Please pass the meat loaf." But we don't stand on formality, which is one of the things I love about us.

I shoveled a forkful of meat loaf into my mouth, closed my eyes as I chewed. Gram's secret ingredient is basil, which, with the onion, creates the most wonderful blend of sweet and savory.

Savory and sweet. Great in meat loaf and great in relationships. I looked at my brother Greg across the table, his wife, Sarah, next to him. They are meat loaf: he's the savory, she's the sweet. Their marriage works. Gram is sweet and sometimes savory. Nathan is also. Meat loaf, definitely.

Billy had been the savory, but so had I at times. Neither one of us was particularly sweet. Maybe we didn't balance each other at all. And we drank a lot back then. Maybe that's why we imploded. Of course, there was his cheating too. Couldn't discount that.

Relationships need balance, sweet and savory, dark and light. I thought about Jillian's white owl tattoo and Jason's black owl. Brother and sister getting matching tattoos? What was the deal with those two? Jillian said hers symbolized purity. But red stilettos? What did those symbolize?

I took the last bite of my meat loaf just as Gram brought dessert to the table. Her coconut custard pie with mile-high meringue, lightly toasted under the broiler.

A perfect ending to a perfect meal.

I pictured Jillian and Jason in that mess of a house—their house now. What would they be having tonight for dinner? I felt a pang of pity for them. Orphaned. At least they had each other.

I let out a sigh and decided I'd done enough thinking for the day. I settled back to enjoy the rest of the evening, letting

Gram's meringue melt on my tongue as I listened to the happy chatter around the table.

My family. Quirky, funny, infuriating. Gotta love 'em.

Well, I don't gotta, but I do.

# CHAPTER TWENTY-EIGHT

## Saturday, November 17

J ILLIAN HAD FOUND THE name and phone number of the man who wanted the helmet. I found his address online. He lived across town from Cliff's house in an area of Three Rivers known as The Bottoms, a stretch of flat land south of town on the eastern bank of the Wolf River.

In the past, most of the area's residents worked at the paper factory on the river. Homes were neat and tidy, with baskets of petunias hanging from front porches. Children played on the sidewalks, safely in the care of family, watched over by their neighbors.

All that changed in the late 1960s. Factory runoff polluted the Wolf River, resulting in astronomical fines from the EPA. The place went bust and closed in the 1970s.

The Bottoms went downhill after that. Workers moved away. A transient population moved in. Most of the assaults, stabbings, and drug dealings in Three Rivers—not that we have a lot—take place in The Bottoms.

I drove Cricket there, doing my best to ignore the chirping. Tony Rislow lived in a small, gray, two-story house with peeling paint and a front yard of clumps of weeds interspersed with bare dirt. A painted sign on a metal frame was stuck in the ground, declaring THIS WAY TO PACKERLAND with an arrow pointing to the left.

I followed the narrow sidewalk to the left around the house.

Tony Rislow's garage was twice the size of an average city garage. Constructed of corrugated steel, the dark green exterior walls sported bands of yellow trim at the corners, around the overhead garage door, the yellow access door, and a small window on the side wall. Packers colors. Above the garage door, another sign, green with yellow lettering, indicated I had, indeed, arrived at PACKERLAND.

The garage was locked up tight. I went to the side door, cupped my hands over my eyes, and peered inside. Across the garage, a wall full of football jerseys under glass in frames. At the far end, I saw what looked like shelves full of football helmets.

A security light blinked from the far corner. I looked up and saw an outside camera. I smiled and waved. *Just a friendly person coming by, curious, maybe interested in buying football stuff. Nothing to be alarmed about. I'll be on my way.*

I turned from the garage, walked nonchalantly back to the car, and headed back to the Victorian. Whatever Tony Rislow had to say would have to wait.

My cell beeped. A text from Tansy:

Wanna go out? 7?

It was Saturday, and my life was a complete bore. I shot back:

YES PLS!!

TANSY AND I MET AT SEVEN at Old Town Tap, a local restaurant with great burgers and a casual vibe. She was dressed in black leggings and a striped, yellow-green-blue long-sleeved top, form-fitting her fit form. Her long blonde hair, with one streak of blue, fell over her shoulders. She looked great, as always.

"Jade's meeting us here," Tansy said.

Jade arrived ten minutes later. I watched her approach. She doesn't walk. She floats. Her long, colorful skirt and loose tunic swirled around her slender frame as she moved.

Jade is a striking beauty. She's five-ten, with graceful limbs, caramel skin from her Jamaican mother, and red highlights in her curly brown hair courtesy of her Irish father. With layers of necklaces and bracelets, and rings on several fingers, her presentation says she is an Artist, with a capital A. And her body is one of her canvasses.

Tansy is fit, Jade is flashy, and I'm, well, just regular. Unspectacular. Ordinary. Fine. Just fine.

Jade had news—a gallery in the city was interested in her work. Her blue eyes sparkled as she filled us in. "I barely make enough to eat, selling a piece here and there and teaching my classes." Jade offers classes through the community education program at Wolf Valley Technical College. "This could be my big break." Jade deserved it.

We toasted her good news, Tansy with a club soda and Jade and me with wine. We'd just dug into our burgers when Tansy, who was facing the door, said, "Isn't that Vince?" I'd told her how he'd asked me to go out.

I turned in my chair. Yep. Vince. With his ex-wife, Lori. She graduated from Three Rivers High with Tansy, Jade, and me.

I turned away, whispered to Tansy. "What are they doing now?"

"They're going to the bar. No, wait, they're coming this way!"

I ducked down. Why, I'm not sure. I chomped into my burger.

"Mackenzie?" Vince said.

I looked up, my mouth full. I tried to say, "Hey Vince," but it came out "Bey Bince" with a side of spit. I wiped at my chin. *Smooth.*

He chuckled, then greeted Tansy and Jade. "You all know Lori?"

We nodded, said the polite things you say. With a "See you later," Vince and Lori walked to another table.

Rational Me explained it. *They're exes. They have history. No big deal.*

I tried to focus on my conversation with Jade and Tansy, but Anxious Me couldn't resist sneaking glances in their direction and going nutso. *They don't have any kids. Why do they even need to talk to each other? Are they getting back together?*

*So much for your romance,* Snarky said.

I wanted another glass of wine, but I was driving. So, I drank sparkling water with a twist of lime and tried not to sulk.

# CHAPTER TWENTY-NINE

I T WAS JUST AFTER eight-thirty that night when we left Old Town Tap. Jade said she needed to get home to work on some pieces for the possible gallery showing.

While standing out by our cars, Tansy said, "I can tell you're really bummed about seeing Vince with his ex."

"Am not!" *Who cares about stupid Vince and his stupid ex? Snarky is evidently still in middle school.*

"Yeah, you are." Tansy was smug, and she was right. I'd had hopes for Vince. Now, I wasn't so sure.

I told her I wanted to see if I could catch Tony Rislow at home, though I wasn't keen on the idea of going to his neighborhood alone after dark.

Tansy offered to ride with me. "You may need backup," she said.

"What will you do? Go all Down Dog on the guy?"

"Hey, I'm stronger than I look," she said. "You'd be surprised how many serious athletes—boxers too—use yoga for building strength. They don't call it Warrior Pose for nothing!"

"How does that work? 'Hold still, please, while I assume my warrior position'?"

She rolled her eyes. "Shut up," she said with a laugh.

Tansy rode shotgun as we drove to The Bottoms. Cricket's crickets were especially crickety, probably because it was dark and, well, you know, crickets.

"Good grief. How can you stand all the noise in here?"

"Yeah. I've got to do something about that."

I filled Tansy in on what was going on with everything and why I wanted to talk to Rislow.

"Oh my God!" she said. "You were in the house, and he was there? What if he'd had a gun or something? What good would a shoe be?"

"Well, in my defense, it *was* a stiletto." But I hadn't thought about him having a gun. My stomach knotted at the possibility.

I parked the car, got out, and looked up and down the street. A few houses down, neighbors were partying on their front lawn. A couple of dogs barked. A pickup with a bad muffler rumbled by.

Tansy walked with me to the back of Rislow's house. The garage was lit up, and the door was open. Rock music wafted out across the backyard.

Tansy looked up at the PACKERLAND sign. "A bit much, don't you think?"

"Yeah, he puts the fanatic in fan."

A man stood at the workbench on the right side of the garage, his back to us. Tallish. Jeans, denim shirt, running shoes spattered with green and yellow paint.

*Way to notice the details in case you have to describe him to the police later.* Rational Me felt proud.

Anxious Me argued, *Police? We should* not *be here. This guy might be a murderer!*

Cans of green and yellow paint stood open on the worktop, brush handles sticking out of them. Packers memorabilia filled every wall and shelf in the garage.

I hollered above the music. "Mr. Rislow?"

He shut off the boombox on the workbench and turned. "That's me," he said with a smile. It sounded like the voice I'd heard at Cliff's, but unless he dropped an F-bomb, I couldn't be certain. "Come on in," he said.

I stepped forward, extending my hand. "My name's Mackenzie Prentice. And this is Tansy Pemberley."

He wiped his hand against his jeans and shook with us. "Tony. People call me Tony." Then he squinted at me and raised his eyebrows. "Have we met?"

*Oh crap. He saw the security footage.* "I stopped by before, but you weren't here. I saw the camera."

Recognition registered on his face. "Oh, sure. That's where I've seen you."

Tansy flashed him a smile and asked, "Do you mind if I look around?"

Tony grinned back. "Feel free!" She walked toward the jerseys framed on the wall. He watched her walk. Most guys seem to appreciate the graceful way Tansy moves her yoga body.

I cleared my throat, and he turned, reluctantly, it seemed, back to me. Plain old me.

I continued. "I'm, um, a relative of Clifford Wilson's." Lying again. I watched his face.

He knit his brows. "Who?"

"My—um, Mr. Wilson is dead." *Oh, wow, this is going splendidly.* I should have left Snarky in the car.

He shrugged. "Don't know the guy."

"You left your name and number. Something about buying a Packers helmet or, rather, buying it back. A helmet your wife sold in a garage sale?"

His mouth twitched. He bit his lower lip, looked down as he nodded. "Oh. Oh, yeah. Yeah. The wife got ticked and sold a bunch of my stuff while I was gone hunting. She had no right to do that."

"Bet that made you mad."

He frowned and gave a snort. "Well, yeah! She had no right!" His shout carried into the night. I was almost a hundred percent sure his was the voice I'd heard at Cliff's.

From behind his back, Tansy shot me a warning frown with a shake of her head as Anxious weighed in. *Geez, you really didn't give much thought to this, did you, getting a potentially violent man riled up?*

I smiled what I hoped was a calming smile and kept my tone casual. "Did you still want the helmet back? Now that my, uh, uncle is gone, we're, uh, divesting. He had quite the collection." It was scary how good I was getting at lying to people.

He eyed me. I imagined his wheels turning. *Does she know?*

I eyed him back as my wheels turned too. *Does he know that I know? Do I really know anything for sure?*

After a long moment, he looked away and shrugged again. "Nah. I'll just let that one go."

I looked past him and pointed at the jerseys with scrawled autographs that had Tansy's attention.

"You've got some collection here. Can I take a closer look?"

"Sure," he said with a grin. He walked toward Tansy. I followed him, noticing a slight limp as he walked.

One jersey in a glass case had number 13 on the back and, above that, the name RISLOW.

Tansy said, "Wow! You played for the Packers?"

"I wish! I played in high school and college. Dreamed of going pro like every kid. Pro scouts showed some interest. But end of the season senior year, I blew out my knee. Busted it up really bad. Missed my chance." He looked at the floor, shaking his head, then gestured toward the jersey. "My wife had that made for me one Christmas. Picked unlucky number 13 as a joke. She laughed about it." He frowned. "I didn't."

"That's terrible!" Tansy said.

"Still bothers you," I said.

"Nah, I'm over it now. What football started, Desert Storm finished for me." He raised his right pant leg, exposing a prosthesis.

"Oh, I'm so sorry."

"Water under the bridge, right? Can't live in the past."

I looked at the far wall where twelve helmets were lined up on shelves, four rows of three. Neat and tidy, polished and shining, reflecting the overhead lights.

I pointed at the display. "Can we take a closer look at the helmets?"

He beamed. "Absolutely!" He led the way. "Got 'em arranged historically, oldest to newest." He pointed to the top left. "That one up there, that was Bart Starr's. Signed his full name on that one. Bryan Bartlett Starr," he said, a note of reverence in his voice. "Worth thousands."

"And this one here," he said, patting the helmet on the bottom right. "This one here was worn by Brett Favre. The Man himself." All the helmets bore signatures of players, with indications of Super Bowl wins or Hall of Fame inductions. "I've been watching the online auctions for a good deal on an Aaron Rodgers helmet. I'm going to have to add more shelves."

Tony Rislow chatted on about who wore which helmet, what they were worth. "Some real treasures out there. You can get good deals if you know what to look for. Turn around and sell the right thing to the right buyer—you can make some serious money."

I wondered if Cliff hoped to make "serious money" from his collections.

I asked, "Aren't you worried about keeping all this out here in the garage? Someone breaking in? Stealing something?"

He pointed toward the ceiling. Sensors. Cameras all around. The garage obviously more important than the house to him. "This place is climate-controlled, and I've got state-of-the-art security here. And the alarm would wake the dead. Nobody's going to be taking anything out of here without a fight."

*Without a fight. Interesting choice of words.*

I didn't see any empty spots on the shelves. "What about the helmet your wife sold? That wasn't part of the display?"

He twitched again, glanced at the ceiling, then met my gaze and shrugged. "Nope. That one didn't really matter much. Didn't care much about that one at all. That's why I'm willing to just let it go."

Hmm. A minute ago, he was furious, and now it was no big deal? I pressed a little further. "But someone heard you arguing with Cliff about it, said you were pretty mad, demanding that he sell it back to you."

His face went stony. "Yeah, well, that was then. I'm over it. Don't care anymore."

I wished with all my might that I could have picked out the helmet on the wall that I'd seen on the dining room table at Cliff's. But I could not. You've seen one green and yellow football helmet, you've seen them all.

"If that's it, I've got to get back to work here," he said, his tone brusque, dismissive.

I wanted to ask him more questions, but Tansy put a hand on my arm. "Thanks for your time," she said, pulling me out of the garage.

I was quiet driving Tansy back to her car. She was animated.

"Oh my gosh, I can see why you love digging into stuff. That was amazing! The way you were questioning him like that and getting him riled up. You hoped he'd say something, like admit he was in Cliff's house, that he stole something, right? That was your plan, wasn't it? So exciting!"

"Yeah." I didn't want to admit I hadn't really had a plan going in. She gushed on about how amazing, exciting, awesome it was—I was—but I was only half listening. The thing that had been niggling in the back of my brain floated to the surface.

I'd taken pictures of Cliff's collections with my phone.

We got to the parking lot at Old Town Tap and sat in the car. Tansy looked on as I scrolled through my photos to the shots of Cliff's dining room.

"What a hoard!" Tansy said.

I pointed at the Packers stuff. There in the pile were the helmets, and on one of the helmets, a partial signature. I zoomed in with my fingers and squinted at the picture.

I could see the end of the handwritten "lett Starr."

"Yes! That's the one that Tony guy was so proud of!" Tansy said.

"Signed by Bart Starr with his full name. Tony said it was worth thousands. But is this helmet the same helmet? Is Tony the guy I heard?"

"The police could dust it for prints," Tansy said, excitement in her voice.

I felt suddenly superior, more experienced in this world of mysteries and solutions. "Tans, what would that prove? That Cliff had the helmet, and now Tony had it. So what? He could say that Cliff sold it to him."

She deflated. "I suppose so, but there was *some* kind of crime here, wasn't there?"

Rational Me answered her. "Bart Starr could have signed a bunch of helmets that way. We can't be sure this is the same helmet. Even if it is, there's nothing to prove he pushed Cliff or anything."

Snarky said, *And think about it, Sherlock. What kind of a crook gives his victim his name and number? Huh?*

Anxious got, well, anxious. *And besides, there's no way to say anything to the police without admitting you were there, upstairs, trespassing! Let this go!*

"There's nothing we can do, really, Tans. He's got the helmet—if it's even the same one. His collection's restored." I thought about his leg. "The guy's been through enough."

"What? Just because the guy's a veteran, he can do what he wants? Break into somebody's house? Take stuff?" Tansy sounded like Heather.

"I'm not saying that. But there's no evidence. We can't be sure of anything."

Tansy gave me a long look. "Well, you're the detective, not me." She smiled, got out of the car, then turned before she shut the door. "You know, we should have thanked him for his service."

Tansy was right. As I drove away, Kinder, Gentler Me decided to just let it go. *Let sleeping dogs lie.*

I ignored Anxious as she whispered, *Any dog will bite if provoked.*

# CHAPTER THIRTY

## Sunday, November 18

G RAM CAME TO MY room early Sunday morning. "Mackenzie? Sweetie? Do you want to come to church with us today?"

I groaned. Chloe, curled up beside me, didn't move a muscle. I didn't want to move either.

Gram continued. "I know it's early, but it would be so lovely to have you there. It's always a special service before Thanksgiving." She patted my arm through the covers.

I didn't want to leave the cozy comfort of the big pink bed. I knew that if I said no, she'd accept that. And I knew that if I said yes, it would make her happy. And who was I to deprive my dear grandmother of a little happiness?

I sat up, raked a hand through my hair, rubbed my eyes, and stretched. "Okay, I'll go with you."

Her grin covered her whole face.

And that's how I ended up that afternoon scooping mashed potatoes onto plates to feed what felt like the entire population of Three Rivers.

The Sunday before Thanksgiving, Our Savior's Lutheran offers a free turkey dinner to the community—all are welcome, no questions asked. Donations are accepted, but anyone can eat for free. I was the mashed potatoes girl, Gram was on gravy duty, and my mother was at the end of the line, dishing out pie.

I noticed a man lingering near my mother, chatting with her. And I noticed an expression I'd never seen on my mother's face.

*What is she doing? Oh. My. Gosh. Is she flirting? No! Can't be? Is she?*

Fascinating. She batted her eyelashes. She giggled. I'm sure I've never heard my mother giggle. She's usually so serious, so anxious. But here she was, tittering and moving her hand toward this guy, as if to say, "Oh, stop! You're embarrassing me."

He seemed to love this bizarre behavior. And the more she pretended to protest, the more he leaned in and whispered things to her. *Whatever. Ew.*

She was eating it up, and I felt confused. My mother? Relationship? What planet were we on? She had been adamantly single, saying stuff like, "I don't have time for all that nonsense!" "This is my time to do what I want!" She was a runner, a knitter, had friends, and worked at the bank. And she helped Gram with caregiving and chores.

She had a life. A full life. She insisted no man was going to ruin that life like my father had when he walked out and left her with us five kids.

So now, what the heck was this? I took a good look at the guy. Tall, not bad looking. Nice smile. Scar across his right cheek, faint but visible from this distance. Clean-shaven. Trim haircut, a little thin on top but nicely salt-and-peppery. No desperate ponytail or man bun. Decent body, from what I could see. Definitely not overweight, no pot belly. Looked to be about my mom's age—sixty-ish.

Romantic Me had questions. *Where did they meet? How long have they been doing this, uh, flirting thing? Have they been secretly dating? Ooh! Maybe they'll run away together.* Romantic Me gets carried away at times.

He moved off to eat his pie. My mother had the weirdest look on her face as she watched him walk away. Wistful, smiling. Another shock to my sensibilities. I couldn't recall the last time my mother looked like that. Happy.

We finished serving the food. The second shift of church volunteers, having finished eating, came into the kitchen to start the cleanup. Gram, my mother, and I took our plates and sat at a table where Nathan had sat with a couple of the men from church. They'd kept him company while we were serving. Now they'd gone into the kitchen for cleanup duty.

"Where have you been?" Nathan asked Gram.

"Working in the kitchen."

"You cooked all day. You should sit down and eat."

Gram patted his arm. "Yes, dear, I'm doing just that." She slid a piece of pie in his direction.

My mother sat silently eating, obviously not present with us. I broke the silence. "So, Mom, who's the mystery man?"

Her head came up quickly, color rising to her cheeks. "What man? I don't know what you're talking about!"

"I saw you flirting," I said with a little tilt of my head back toward the buffet line.

She blushed deeper. "I was not flirting!"

"Sure looked like flirting to me."

Gram joined in. "What guy? What are you talking about?" She looked around the dining hall. "Where is he? Who is it?"

I gestured with my head. "Don't look, but he's sitting over by the windows."

Which, of course, made Gram look. She gave him a little wave, and he waved back. Gram said, loud enough for the whole room to hear, "Ooh, he's good-looking, Barbara!"

My mom got even redder and grabbed Gram's arm. "Shush! It's nothing! Stop!"

We didn't stop, of course, until she told us that he—Duncan was his name—was someone she'd worked with at the shoe factory back when I was in high school. She was a bookkeeper in the office, and he was one of the managers. She said they hadn't seen each other for years, and then here he was. He'd lost his wife a couple of years ago, felt the need to reconnect with his spiritual roots, was visiting churches in town, and just happened to be here at Our Savior's today.

I frowned at her. "No way, Mom. What I saw there between you two was definitely not in the we-just-ran-into-each-other-today category. What's the real story?"

She blushed, cleared her throat, and confessed. That story she'd just handed us was, indeed, a big fat lie. She and Duncan had been dating on the sly for several weeks.

"Why didn't you tell us?" Gram sounded a little hurt.

"Because I didn't want this third degree. This family! Ugh!" And with that, she took her pie and coffee and left us. We watched her walk across the room to Duncan's table. He stood and pulled out a chair for her.

Romantic Me liked that a lot. *Aw, how sweet. So chivalrous. Maybe someday I'll find someone like that.*

Snarky Me piped up. *Seriously? You're jealous of your mother. Pathetic.*

Pathetic Me couldn't argue with that.

Gram and I turned in our chairs to stare at the two of them. "Well, I never thought I'd live to see this," Gram said.

"Me neither. My mom has a boyfriend."

"A gentleman caller."

"A boy toy."

"A suitor."

"A significant other," I said.

"Ooh, maybe he's her *luh-ver*," said Gram.

"Ew!" said I. "That's just too weird!"

Gram smiled. "Not weird. Your mother deserves to be happy, and you can see there's some potential here. Can't you feel it?"

Pathetic Me had a moment there. *Wow. It's been so long since you had anything with anybody, you don't even recognize the signals.*

I'd had a few heart-racing pitty-pats here and there, but since the long-ago, early days with Billy, I hadn't had any real connection, nothing life-changing. I'd had a few dates: with Kyle, who left me for Bangladesh or maybe for some guy in a Peter Pan costume, and one date with a guy named Frank. And checking out an arson scene with Vince wasn't exactly rom-com material.

So yeah, it had been a long, long time. I was overdue for some romance in my life.

Every part of me agreed with that.

# CHAPTER THIRTY-ONE

## Still Sunday

W E WERE READY TO head home when Lou hollered at us from across the church narthex. "Virginia! I found it!"

Gram and I exchanged a look. Hard telling what Lou might have found in her stash of stuff. She fast-walked our way.

"I found your missing brooch!" Lou was breathing hard, excited.

"What do you mean 'missing'?" Gram turned to me, surprise turning to accusation in her look. *Oops.* I hadn't told Gram the brooch had been stolen. "Mackenzie? What happened to the brooch?"

I filled Gram in quickly, and Lou interrupted. "Never mind how it got missing. I found it! I was just at the nursing home, visiting my cousin Gert. You remember her, don't you, Virginia? She used to be a blackjack dealer in Las Vegas, then she married that guy who was—"

I held up a hand. "Lou, the brooch?"

"Oh, sorry. Yes, I was there at Drury's Rest visiting Gert, and this old woman comes down the hall with her walker. She's wearing your pin, big as you please!"

"How can you be sure it was my pin?" Gram asked.

"Are you kidding? That gorgeous thing is one of a kind! Never saw another one like it! I'd recognize it anywhere."

I left Lou to her delusion that our humble family was somehow in possession of a great treasure instead of a cheap imitation.

She went on. "The old gal said her sister gave it to her. I asked at the desk who she was and where I might find this sister. The nurse tells me the old lady doesn't have a sister, but her granddaughter visits every week, and that's who brought her the pin."

"Does this granddaughter have a name?" I asked.

"The nurse said Lily, I think, or maybe it was Libby. The girl comes on Wednesday and Sunday every week like clockwork, right around four, to have dinner with her grandma at four-thirty. She's late twenties with spikey pink hair. 'Can't miss her,' the nurse said. So maybe you can catch her and ask her about the brooch?"

Gram looked at her wristwatch, then at me. "It's three-thirty right now. Perfect time for a stakeout."

I shook my head. "No, Gram. The pin went missing on my watch, so I'll be the one to retrieve it. Besides, it's been a long day already, hasn't it? I'll go next Wednesday."

Gram's turn to shake her head. "What's wrong with you? A long day? What are you—an old lady?"

*Geez, she really is the Energizer Bunny.* My cheeks got hot. "Aren't *you* tired?"

"Nope! I want that brooch back, so let's get over there right now. I'll be your whatchamacallit—your wingman! I'll say I'm visiting a friend. Remember Mrs. Connolly? She's at Drury's now."

Our former neighbor Mrs. Connolly always had the best candy at Halloween, handing out full-size Snickers, not just the little ones.

"Fine. Let's go, Wing Gram."

Gram shot me a smug smile. She loves to get her way. The plan was set. The girl with the spikey pink hair was the thief. I just knew it.

# CHAPTER THIRTY-TWO

M Y MOTHER TOOK NATHAN home after church, leaving Gram and me free to, as Gram put it, "snag us a jewel thief." At Drury's Rest, Gram's shoes squeaked on the linoleum as she headed down the hall to visit Mrs. Connolly. I took a seat in the lobby.

I tried to look casual, just a person waiting for another person. Nothing going on here, people. Not a would-be detective staking out the place. Nope. Just me. Casual.

I flipped through a tattered large print edition of *Reader's Digest*. Does every old person in America love that magazine? Gram's subscribed for decades, and every bathroom in the Victorian has a stash of *Reader's Digest* for your reading pleasure as you sit.

The front door opened, and I saw her. Spikey pink hair, twenty-something. She bounced in and gave a friendly "Hey, how ya doin'?" to the nurse at the front desk. The nurse spoke and nodded in my direction. Spikey came to me, a quizzical look on her face. Spikey wore faded, tattered jeans and a blue tee shirt with a picture of a cat saying, "CHECK ME-OWT." Layered over the tee? My favorite shirt with the tell-tale ink stain. *Grr.*

"Do I know you?" she asked.

I shook my head. "I'm Mackenzie. That's a nice shirt." I gave her my most admiring, innocent look. "Where'd you get it?"

She smiled. "My boyfriend got it for me." She ran her hand down the sleeve. "It's super soft. So comfy."

*Yeah. It is. And get your hands off it.*

I noticed then that she was wearing a necklace—a dozen or so small interlocking silver circles—just like one I'd bought at Target a year before. "That's a great necklace. Boyfriend give you that too?"

She frowned. "Yeah. Why do you ask?"

I cleared my throat. "Well, because I had a necklace just like that. And because you gave your grandma a brooch—"

She looked confused. "What's a *brooch*?"

"A brooch is a pin, and I saw the fancy one you gave to your grandma the other day."

"That pin is so pretty, isn't it? My boyfriend found it in a box in the alley. Can you believe it? This shirt was in there and the necklace too. I guess somebody just threw it all out."

"Did he say where—which alley—he found this box?"

"Nope." She frowned. "What's the diff? It was just a box of old stuff."

I wanted to tell her how I felt about all that "old stuff," but I bit my tongue. I decided to tell her the truth. "Look . . ." I almost called her Spikey. "What's your name?"

"Lydia."

"Well, Lydia, here's the deal. My apartment was robbed, and someone stole that shirt and the necklace you're wearing. And the brooch, uh, that pin you gave your grandma, means a lot to me, to my whole family. I'm just trying to figure out who stole it and get it back."

She straightened up, her eyes wide. "You don't think it was Riker!"

"Riker? That's your boyfriend?"

She got flustered. "No, no, that's not his name!" I shot her a look that told her it was no use trying to lie. She stammered, "I mean he—Riker couldn't have—he wouldn't!"

"Has Riker stolen things before?"

"No way! Well, I mean, he did stuff as a kid and was in juvie, but he's good now. He's good! He found the box in the alley, and I believe him!"

"Okay, Lydia, I'm sure he's a great guy," I said, then continued, standing taller, hands on my hips and voice as firm and authoritative as I could make it. "But the fact is that you are in possession of stolen property, and I'm sure you don't want to get in trouble for that. Just return it to me, and I won't *press charges*." I emphasized the last two words, impressing myself with my cop imitation. *Badass. Maybe we should join the force.*

She went pale. Her lower lip trembled as she took off the shirt and necklace and handed them to me. She said she'd go to her grandmother's room and retrieve the brooch.

As I waited for her to come back, I thought. This guy, Riker, may or may not be a thief. Maybe he did find the box in the alley behind Lou's, or maybe he put it there after he robbed me. I didn't have the wherewithal to track him down or the authority to question him, but I knew someone who did.

I texted Heather and asked her to call me back.

I looked up and saw Lydia coming back, an older woman with a walker coming fast behind her, yelling, "Stop! Give me my pin!"

Lydia handed me the brooch and turned to her grand-mother. "Nana, the pin belongs to this lady." *Lady? Why didn't she just call me 'Ma'am'? Ugh.*

"No! It's mine!" Nana hollered and thumped her walker against the tile floor. "Help! Help!"

The front desk nurse trotted over. "What's the trouble, Sylvia?"

The old lady pointed at me. "She's stealing my pin!" I explained the situation, and Lydia confirmed it. I held the neck-lace toward Lydia. "Maybe your grandmother would accept this as a token of my appreciation?"

Lydia took it, showed her grandmother, and lied. "This is worth way more than that old pin, Nana!" I guess a lot of family members learn to tell fiblets.

Nana reached forward and touched the silver circles ten-derly, then smiled as Lydia looped the necklace around her neck. Bringing a hand to the necklace, the old woman said, "I'm so glad to have this back. I lost it years ago, and I've wondered whatever happened to it." She smiled at Lydia. "Your grandfa-ther gave me this necklace for our anniversary. I think it was our thirtieth. Or maybe our fortieth. So many years. So many years."

Lydia smiled that sad smile Gram had at times, and I nod-ded understanding as she turned to escort her grandmother back to her room. Nana and Nathan had a lot in common.

Gram came into the lobby then, and I filled her in as we headed back to the Victorian.

"Do you think this Riker person is the thief?"

"Maybe, maybe not," I said. As I parked the Buick in Gram's garage, Heather called. I gave her the story. She said she was familiar with Riker.

HEATHER CALLED ME BACK JUST BEFORE dinner that night. "Riker says he found the box in the alley behind Lou's Vintage. Said he checks that alley often, along with dumpster diving. Sees nothing wrong with going through and taking, and I quote, 'the shit people throw out.' He takes anything he thinks has street value. With nothing else to go on, we have to assume that's what happened."

Lou was not happy when I called to tell her this. "What kind of lowlife steals from donation boxes? It's like taking money from the collection plate at church!"

I didn't want to remind Lou that she runs a business, not a charity. She was entitled to her opinion and entitled to her decision to install security cameras and motion-sensitive flood lights in the alley behind the store.

# CHAPTER THIRTY-THREE

JUST BEFORE SUNDOWN ON Sunday afternoon, I went cricket hunting. Armed with a can of Raid and a flyswatter, I opened all the doors of the Escape, which was parked behind the Victorian. Chloe sat on the driveway behind me, curious, her tail on high alert twitching slowly back and forth.

I leaned into the car and listened. Nary a chirp. "Where are you, you little buggers?"

Silence. I chuckled, thinking how people talk about hearing crickets when there's no response. "Where are you now that I want to hear you?"

I swept the flyswatter under the front passenger seat. Checked the floor. Opened the back hatch. Swept under the driver's seat. My efforts yielded some old french fries, a couple of dried-up apple slices, and some candy wrappers. No crickets.

I closed the car doors, looked at Chloe. "Well, girl, I guess they live to chirp another day. Or maybe they escaped the Escape." I chuckled. Chloe didn't. She headed into the house, and I followed.

turned off the lights on the main floor. My mother was out with Duncan. Gram and Nathan were upstairs in bed.

I was heading up to bed myself when Gram's front doorbell rang. I looked through the wavery glass and saw the shapes of two people standing a few feet back from the door.

"Who is it?" I asked, cell phone in hand, ready to call 911 if needed.

"Are you Mackenzie Prentice?" Man's voice, deep.

"Who's asking?"

I heard a muffled exchange of words and then another voice, not as deep. "Riker Schmitt. I need to talk to you."

I slipped my cell into my pocket and opened the door a crack. In the glow of the porch light, Riker stood staring at his feet. Early twenties, I judged, stringy hair, wearing a Packers jersey, multiple ear piercings. Behind him stood an older man in dark blue coveralls, the kind auto mechanics sometimes wear.

The older man spoke as he shoved Riker forward. "My son here had a visit from the police earlier. Handed them a pile of horseshit, which he has since cleared up with them. Now he has something to say to you, don't you, Riker?"

Head down, he started to say, "I'm sorry . . ." Riker's father punched him on the shoulder. "Look at the lady!" *Lady? Again? Geez, Louise! How old did people think I was?*

Riker raised his eyes to meet mine, and I noticed a bruise on his left cheek. I winced, hoping that bruise hadn't come from his father.

"I'm sorry, ma'am," Riker stammered. *Ma'am? Ugh.*

His father thumped him on the shoulder again. "Speak up, idiot!"

Riker cleared his throat and spoke louder as he fixed me with a look. Was it defiant? Or pleading? I couldn't quite read it. "I'm sorry that I took your stuff."

His father barked. "Tell her the whole goddamn story!"

Riker sighed and looked down again. "I broke in after the fire. I took everything I thought I could sell. Clothes, jewelry."

I felt anger rising. "And my shoes? You thought you could sell those?"

"I gave all the shoes to this homeless woman I know. I didn't know what else to do with those. They were pretty beat up."

That earned Riker another slug from his dad. "Don't disrespect the lady's stuff!" he barked, then said to me, "He's going to have to go to court, pay for what he done, don't worry about that." He gave his son another shove. "Go ahead, finish up so the lady can get to sleep."

"Sorry. Sorry for any problem I caused you," Riker said as if he'd practiced the line. "And Lydia told me about you getting your pin back. I would have sold that, but it was pretty, and I thought Lydia's gran would like it."

Aw, Riker had a soft spot for grandmothers. "That was sweet of you, sort of," I said. Riker looked so surprised by that comment that I wondered if he ever heard anything positive about himself. Not likely from his father.

I cleared my throat. "Well, I appreciate you coming here, Riker. It takes courage to own up to this kind of thing." I said this loudly for his father's benefit. I wanted the old man to know that someone saw something decent in his kid, even though he'd screwed up.

His dad tugged on the back of Riker's shirt. "Let's go," he said, then turned to me as they headed down the porch steps. "He won't bother you again."

I called after them. "Thanks, Riker. You did the right thing!"

I closed the door. Should I have said something about the bruise on Riker's face? Was it something to tell Heather about? I couldn't be sure his father had caused it.

Besides, Riker was an adult, and adults have options.

Don't they?

# CHAPTER THIRTY-FOUR

### Monday, November 19

I WALKED INTO THE KITCHEN just after eight on Monday morning. My mother and Gram were finishing breakfast. My mom was dressed for work in gray wool slacks topped with a gorgeous pale blue cashmere sweater she'd snagged from Stephanie's pile. Gram was in a lime green velour tracksuit—a Lou's Vintage find, no doubt.

They were in the middle of something. My mom said, "I don't need you giving Duncan the third degree. We're too old for that 'meet the parents' stuff."

Gram huffed. "Oh, so you're too old for good manners?"

"You know what I mean. It's awkward, that scrutiny. Nobody likes that kind of thing."

Gram said, "Sounds like he's a teenager, so nervous about meeting a girl's parents. Is he that insecure? Immature? Is that it?"

*Ooh.* Gram was playing one of her little tricks. When I was a kid, I didn't want to try broccoli. Gram said, "Well, if you're not *brave enough* to try it . . ." as she started to take the plate away.

I pulled the plate back. "I am *too* brave enough!" Tricks like that always worked on us kids, but it was impressive to see Gram working my mother the same way.

Gram asked again, "Is that it? He's like a nervous teenage boy?"

"Absolutely not!" My mother stood, paused, then sighed. Her shoulders slumped. "Fine. I'll ask him to come to lunch." She put her plate and cup a little too firmly into the sink and left for work.

Gram shot me a triumphant look. "Well, how 'bout that? That trick still works." She winked at me as she said, "When Duncan comes to lunch, we'll have broccoli."

Tricky. Very tricky.

I finished my breakfast while Gram loaded the crockpot with a whole chicken, sliced carrots, and chopped onions. She poured in some chicken broth, ground in some pepper, and tossed in a palmful of dried basil. My mouth watered in anticipation of tonight's dinner.

I checked my phone. It was almost nine-thirty. I asked Gram, "What time are you leaving for coffee at Hilda's?"

"The girls aren't meeting this morning," she said. "Velma's sister is in town for Thanksgiving, and Estelle has the flu, so I'll be home here with Nathan."

"Okay. If you don't need me, I've got some errands to run before I go to Lou's."

"No problem. See you later."

Lou expected me at the shop around noon. I planned to head over to Cliff's, get inside, and snoop through the basement.

I steered Cricket down the alley and called my mother, who assured me Jillian was at work again. I assumed Jason was teaching. I had a good two hours.

I parked a block away from Cliff's, took my mini flashlight from the glove compartment, slipped it and my cell into the pocket of my hooded sweatshirt. I pulled the hood up to hide my face and walked to the house.

No neighbors in sight, I went around to the back door. Skipped the pretense of knocking. The door was unlocked. I slipped inside.

Silence. I called up the stairs just in case Jason had taken a sick day or something. If he'd been there, I'd have had to think fast.

More silence. I did a quick walk through the first floor. Nothing had changed since the other day. I said hello to Brett and assiduously avoided the spot where I'd uncovered the dead whatever-that-was.

I walked back into the kitchen and was on the top step heading into the basement when I heard a male voice behind me. "Stop! Put your hands up! Do it now!"

Heart in my throat, I put my hands up and stammered, "I'm not—I don't—"

"Turn around slowly," he said.

I turned to face Officer Burns. Well, actually, his gun. Second time in a month I was on the wrong end of a firearm. A quiver ran through me, head to toe.

Recognition registered on his face. "Oh, it's you." He holstered the weapon, then keyed his shoulder mike and said, "Clear in here."

A moment later, Heather Sullivan walked in. She did not look happy to see me. "Mackenzie? What are you doing here?"

I shrugged. She frowned, shook her head, then turned to Burns. "Pat down?"

He shook his head.

"Turn around," she told me. I obeyed. She ran her hands down my body as she hissed in my ear. "What the *hell* are you doing here?"

I hissed back. "You told me to!"

"I most certainly did not!"

"But that feather—"

"Oh, for the love of—" She finished patting me and used her normal voice. "Okay, put your hands down." I did, and we both turned around.

Heather said, "I've got this, Burns. You can leave. She's a friend of, um, the homeowner. I'll take it from here."

Burns left. Heather scowled. "Okay, spill. What the hell were you thinking? The neighbor called us. Said some creeper in a hoodie was skulking around the house. Thought you might be a burglar. You aren't, are you?"

"A creeper? Nope."

"A burglar?" She raised her eyebrows.

"No. Of course not," I said, though I figured I was skating mighty close to the legal definition of the term.

Heather pressed on. "Okay, so explain why you're here then."

Anxious Me went into high gear. *What* are *we doing here? Snooping where we don't belong. Playing detective. Make some excuse and get out!*

Rational Me scrambled for an answer that wouldn't get me in trouble. "Um, my grandmother, well, uh, she, uh, I just wanted to see if I could figure out how Cliff died."

"For God's sake, Mackenzie. We know how. He fell. Hit his head. Died."

"But what about the feather?"

"You and the damn feather! What about it? Jesus, look around. He could have inhaled all kinds of things!"

"But there's no sign of a birdcage here. I talked to the next-door neighbors and—"

"You did what?" Her voice rose. "Why?"

"Because Jason said he heard Cliff yelling at someone the day he died. And there was a long-standing feud with the guy next door."

She shot a look out the kitchen window at the Crandall house. "You had no business snooping around like that," she said in a harsh whisper.

I hissed, "Like what? I have every right to talk to people!"

The whisper-fight continued, even though we were alone in the house. Heather said, "What if the neighbor *did* do something, and what if your talking to him screwed up the case? I told you to let me know if you discovered anything, didn't I? And you promised you would!"

I hissed back, "I couldn't screw up the case because there *wasn't* any case! You guys closed the file, figured some old guy fell down and died. I just thought it was worth checking out, that's all."

She gave me a long look, then took a deep breath, let out a grunt of disgust, and shook her head. In her regular voice, she said, "Okay, fair enough. Start at the beginning. How did you get in?"

I didn't think it was a good idea to tell her I'd been in the house before. "The back door was open."

She frowned. "Open? Did you turn the doorknob to get in?"

"It was open." Now, she and I obviously had different definitions for our words here.

She asked for clarification. "*Was* it open or did *you* open it?"

"I knocked. It opened. I swear. I *entered*, yes, but I didn't *break*."

"Still a crime. Unauthorized entering."

Huh. You learn something every day.

Heather took me by the elbow, started to steer me toward the back door. "Let's go."

I resisted, planted my feet. "But you're a cop. *You* have every right to be here. The neighbor called."

"Well, *I* have the right, but you definitely *do not*. Now come on, or I'll have to arrest you!"

I gave her a pleading look. "Can we just look around a little bit? There's nothing upstairs except a couple of bedrooms that are really neat and clean. As in creepy neat and clean." I let her assume I'd been up there before she arrived that day. No need to tell her about my previous visit. Or about the guy I was ready to hit with the stiletto. "The only other place I haven't looked is the basement. I was about to go down there when you arrived."

She frowned. I pressed. "Pretty please? I won't touch anything. Just five minutes in the basement? That's all I'm asking. Just five measly minutes."

She stared at me, considering, then blew out a breath. "I could get in trouble for this but go ahead. You have five minutes. I'll wait up here, but if you find anything down there, you'd better holler." She pulled a pair of black nitrile gloves from a pocket in her duty belt. "Put these on, but don't touch anything. Got it?"

I shot her a grin. She rolled her eyes, shaking her head. I went to the top of the basement stairs, flicked on the light switch, and headed down.

# CHAPTER THIRTY-FIVE

T HE BASEMENT WAS A lot like the upstairs, with boxes and clutter to the max and a single path winding through the piles. The smell of mold and mildew made my nose itch. No stench of dead things. *Whew.*

I saw a workbench to the left. I went to it and pulled the chain for the fluorescent fixture hanging above it. The light buzzed, then flickered to life. The workbench was piled high with unfinished projects. Looked like birdhouses or feeders to me.

I followed the path through the stacks. I passed boxes labeled in black marker: BOOKS. KOREA. MOTHER. And lots of boxes marked as MISC. I cringed. My organized mind knows that labeling too many containers MISC is a recipe for disaster.

I paused at a spot where several boxes had toppled over, contents spilled on the path. *Boxes fell. No big deal. Unless someone was pushed into the boxes.* I set the thought aside and stepped over the pile.

At the far wall, a wooden door stood ajar, an open padlock hanging from the latch. I shined my little flashlight into a small, windowless room, maybe five-by-five feet square. The Victorian had a space like this in the basement. Gram called it "the root cellar." A worktable stood against the far wall, shelves of jars and beakers above it, and, on the worktop, a Bunsen burner and various tools for measuring and stirring.

Jason had a chemistry lab down here, a space for working outside of school. *Perfectly innocent, just a science teacher doing lesson prep. No big deal.*

Anxious Me had another opinion. *He's a drug dealer! Cooking meth! I don't know how any of that stuff works, but I'm sure there's criminal stuff going down.* That part of me doesn't let a lack of knowledge stand in the way of jumping to conclusions.

I thought I'd better let Heather know, just in case Anxious was right. I went to the bottom of the stairs. "Hey, Heather, I might have found something!"

I heard her muttering as she came down the steps. ". . . probably nothing . . . waste of time . . . pain in the . . . What is it?"

I led her to the back room, shining my little flashlight inside. "What do you think? Meth lab?"

Snarky scoffed. *What do you know about meth labs?*

Heather pulled out her massive flashlight. Its beam dwarfed mine. She swept the light over the table and shelves. "Jason's a science teacher, right?"

"Yup."

"Then this is like his home office. Makes perfect sense, doesn't it?"

"I suppose. Don't you want to call in CSI to be sure?"

She snorted. "I'm sure enough." Heather had probably seen enough meth labs to know this wasn't one. "Besides, Three

Rivers doesn't have a CSI. You've been watching too much TV. Is that all you found?" she asked, heading for the steps.

I put a hand on her sleeve. She looked at my hand. "Ahem!" she said, giving me a look that implied touching her might be an arrestable offense.

"Oops. Sorry," I said, letting go. "But look here." She followed me to the overturned boxes. "Something happened here."

She scoffed. "Like maybe someone got dizzy and fell? No crime in that."

I pressed the point. "Or maybe someone had a fight. Maybe someone got pushed and fell into the boxes."

Heather paused, then shook her head. "Nope. More logical to assume someone got dizzy here, just like he got dizzy upstairs."

She was still playing that same "dizzy old man" tune. I approached the mess and started shifting boxes, looking behind stacks.

Heather was in the middle of a reprimand, "Hey, I told you not to touch—" when I saw what I was looking for.

"Um, Officer Sullivan? You might want to take a look over here."

A birdcage lay on its side, and around it? Feathers. Lots of little feathers. And two canaries, very yellow and very dead.

# CHAPTER THIRTY-SIX

HEATHER AIMED HER FLASH at the cage. "I'll be damned," she said, and then said it again, "Well, I'll be good and damned."

"Mrs. Crandall next door told me Cliff's wife, Florence, had canaries that died ages ago," I said. "These look like they were just singing yesterday."

"Two dead canaries down here in the dark. Why? Who? What the hell?"

"Do you suppose Cliff got them in his wife's honor? Maybe he kept them down here because Jillian or Jason didn't like their singing?"

"Who doesn't like canaries?" Heather said. "What kind of sick person would stick them down here in this dark, nasty basement?"

"I know! I'd never treat my parakeets like this," I said.

"We had a cockatoo when I was a kid." She got quiet, looked at the ceiling.

"Well, I can't imagine that Cliff would have put them down here. Mrs. Crandall told me how he built feeders and birdhouses because his wife loved birds." I gestured toward the workbench. "Probably abandoned those projects when his wife died."

"That's so sad," Heather said, shaking her head. "But it doesn't explain how these birds ended up down here."

I thought a moment. "Maybe he got the birds to remind him of his wife. You know how when someone dies, the other person wants to hold on to everything? You saw upstairs. That's what's going on here, don't you think?"

Heather nodded. "Yeah, we walk into enough hoarding situations. You just know that something is going on, emotionally or psychologically, with that person."

"So maybe somebody in the house—Jillian or Jason—got annoyed. Maybe Cliff put them down here to keep the peace and forgot about them?" Rational Me whispered, *Not likely.*

But Heather was running with it. "Okay, so going with your theory, let's recreate the scenario." She went to the bottom of the steps. "Say Cliff brought the birds down here." She walked forward, pretending to carry a birdcage. "He sets them down. Maybe he forgets about them. Maybe they starved. Whatever. They die." She made a croaking sound.

I cringed. "Oh, geez. That's awful."

She nodded and continued. "Then maybe he remembered, came back, saw the birds. Got upset, got dizzy, fell, knocked the cage over." She tilted toward the cage, waved her hands upward. "Feathers go flying. He inhales one."

She stopped and knit her eyebrows together. "But how did he not notice that feather? Wouldn't he have sneezed or something? I sure as hell would!"

"Maybe when we get old, we're less sensitive to sensations

like heat, cold?" I told Heather how Gram complains that Nathan wants the heat blasting in the house all winter. "She says her inner thermostat works just fine, but his has gone, as she says, 'whackadoodle.'"

Heather shook her head. "Hot and cold, sure, but not noticing feathers up your nose? Seems a little extreme."

I agreed. I was pretty sure Nathan would still be able to tell if he inhaled a feather. With that thought came a little glimmer of an idea. "What if Cliff didn't have time to notice the feather? What if he was down here, inhaled it, and then someone killed him."

Heather gave a snort. "What are you talking about? Jason found him unresponsive by the fireplace." She stopped, and I picked up the thread.

"Or did he? We only have his word for that, right?"

"No. No. No. He still had a pulse. I checked that myself, and he was breathing when they transported him to the hospital."

"Well, forget that theory, then. He was alive when he was down here, inhaling feathers. What the heck *did* happen?"

We stood in silence for a bit as I looked around the boxes that had tumbled. Shards of broken china cups littered the concrete floor. I shone my flashlight down on pieces of painted hummingbirds and chickadees.

Then I noticed something sticking out from under a box. A thick piece of metal pipe, several inches long.

"Take a look here, Heather."

She bent over to see where I had pointed the light. "Hmm. That could have been there for years, but don't touch it. Hold my flashlight." I trained both beams on the area while she took pictures with her phone of the cage, the boxes around it, and the pipe on the floor.

I felt excitement rise. "It's a metal pipe, right?"

"Yes, it looks to be a metal pipe."

"And that's a dark spot on the floor, right?"

"Yup. Metal pipe. Dark spot."

"Don't you see? This must be the murder weapon, and that spot is blood! Somebody bashed Cliff here! This could be a crime scene!"

Heather took me by the shoulders, pulling me to face her. "Stop right there! No crime scene here. We know the man was still breathing upstairs. Hit his head on the fireplace. Not hit with a pipe. I know that. Personally. I. Was. There. Do you understand?"

I nodded, felt the air leaving my balloon, the rain drenching my parade. Defeated, I said, "Fine. So, what's the pipe doing here?"

"It's a basement. That's a pipe. Look around. There could be anything in this mess, and it would have nothing to do with Cliff's death."

"But two dead canaries in a basement?"

She thought a second, nodded. "Yeah, okay, I'll give you that. The bird thing is weird."

"Okay, great. What do we do now?"

Heather said, "We go upstairs—" She made her fingers walk. "—before someone comes home." She pulled the string to turn off the workbench light, then started up the stairs as I chattered behind her.

"We've found evidence, right? Don't you think you'll open an investigation?"

She spoke over her shoulder. "Nope. This counts for nothing because I'm here without any authorization other than to check the premises because the neighbor called—" She stopped mid-sentence, looking down. "Wait. What's this?"

She pointed her flashlight at the steps. I looked down at several dark spots on the wooden treads. I held the flash while she snapped more pictures.

I wasn't going to risk another shameful reprimand for running away with myself. "Could be mud. Or dog poo. Or paint. Or coffee."

She turned to me. "It could be blood."

Be still my heart.

# CHAPTER THIRTY-SEVEN

S TANDING BY THE STOVE in Cliff's kitchen, I said, "Okay, how about this scenario: Cliff gets some new canaries in honor of his late wife. Somebody doesn't like the birds, puts the cage in the basement. Cliff goes looking for the birds. Somebody hits him with the pipe. They chase him upstairs, maybe, getting blood on the steps without realizing it, shove him, and Cliff hits the fireplace hearth. The rest we know."

Heather considered this. "What's the motive? 'Your canaries are annoying'?"

"Okay, maybe Cliff was down here, and the guy next door came down, fought with him, and then chased him upstairs?"

Heather shrugged.

I was on a roll. "Or how about this? Some random thief came looking for treasures, and Cliff caught them down there. Fight ensued?" Even as I said it, I had trouble imagining Cliff having the strength to fight someone.

She shrugged again.

I had a thought I didn't want to have, hesitated to share it. I swallowed hard. "Jason and Jillian were on all his accounts, and they get the house now."

"And you know this how?" Heather waited.

I didn't want to get my mother in any trouble, so I didn't mention the whole bank thing and the amount in Cliff's account. I lied. "Jillian told me. That's motive, right?"

Heather shook her head. "Cliff obviously trusted them, and if they were on the accounts, they could help themselves to whatever he had. Why kill him?"

"Maybe to avoid the expense of nursing home care down the road?"

She looked skeptical. "Thin. Very thin."

She was obviously just going to shoot down every idea I had. I asked, "So what do we do next?"

"What *we* do now is *we* get out of this house. Then *you* go home, and I go back to the station, let my captain decide if he thinks anything more needs to be done. If there is some reason to take further action, *we*—as in the *police*—will do that. If not, you are going to accept 'case closed' and swear on your mother's life that you will stop snooping around. Deal?"

I nodded. Snarky Me snarked. *Good thing she didn't make you swear on Gram's life. That would be much stronger motivation to butt out.*

Kinder, Gentler Me wanted to slap Snarky for that.

# CHAPTER THIRTY-EIGHT

W E STEPPED OUTSIDE AND were headed to the front of the house just as Bess Crandall came outside. I waved. She waved back, then headed toward us, saying, "Officer, I'm so sorry. I had no idea it was Mackenzie—Cliff's family—in the house, or I never would have bothered the police."

Heather gave me raised eyebrows. I gave her a shrug. *Who me? Letting the Crandalls think I was a relative of Cliff's? Just a little white lie, right?*

Heather smiled at Bess as she joined us in Cliff's front yard. "It's okay. Better safe than sorry. Don't ever hesitate to call." Heather turned to me. "I'll call you later about that, uh, thing we discussed."

I nodded, and Heather left. Bess walked me to my car. She said, "I'm glad to have a chance to talk with you. The other day, I couldn't say anything in front of my husband, but he and Cliff had a terrible argument that day Clifford was found. Both of them yelling. Just terrible."

"Where was this argument?"

"On Clifford's front porch."

"Not inside?" Jason had said he heard an argument inside the house, but with his music playing, he could have been mistaken.

"No, they were outside. I could hear every word because I was out in the front getting my flower beds ready for winter. You know it's so important to put the garden to bed in the fall so you're ready for spring, especially with dahlias—"

I held up a hand and prompted her back on track. "You heard them arguing?"

"Oh, yes. Howard asked Clifford about selling us the place. Clifford just, well, he went ballistic. He yelled, 'Get off my porch!' and pushed Howard. Howie swore and put him in a headlock. Cliff swung and kicked, both of them swearing up a storm. I couldn't believe it! Two old men fighting like that!"

"Sounds awful!"

"It was. Finally, I yelled," she said, putting her fists on her hips, "'Howard Melvin Crandall! You come home this instant, or I'm calling the police!'"

She had that look of satisfaction I'd seen on my mother's face when she sent us kids to our rooms for fighting. "What happened then?"

"Howard knew I was serious. He let Cliff go and headed home, yelling something about how he couldn't wait to go to Cliff's funeral. And Cliff hollered, 'Over my dead body!' Isn't that just terrible? They'd argued before, but this was the worst one ever. I'm surprised Howard didn't have a stroke—"

She gasped. "You don't suppose—" Her eyes filled with tears as her hands went to her cheeks. She met my eyes. "Oh, dear. That's not . . . their fight couldn't have . . . Oh no, no, no.

Tell me that's not what killed Clifford! He didn't have some kind of stroke because of that fight! How could we ever live with ourselves if that's what caused his death? Oh dear. That poor man."

I patted her arm. "I'm sure that wasn't it," I said, but I wasn't a hundred percent certain.

She shook her head, then hugged herself. "Howard was so angry. He spit and spewed for a couple of hours. It wasn't until after we'd had our supper that he finally calmed down. I was so upset, I hardly slept at all that night."

"I can imagine. How is your husband now?"

Bess Crandall frowned, shook her head. "When Clifford died, I thought Howard would feel bad then, but you know, he doesn't. He seems, um, relieved. Not happy, of course, but relieved." She shook her head again, letting out a sigh. "I feel like I don't really know him anymore. This whole feud with Clifford just changed him."

She gave me a head tilt and a sad smile. "Again, I'm so sorry for your loss. Clifford was a good friend, once upon a time."

She said she had to go fix lunch and assured me she'd let me know if she thought of anything else.

As I got into the Escape, I said out loud, "Well, wasn't that interesting?"

Nobody answered. "Ah, the figurative crickets," I said.

A literal cricket chirped back.

I checked my phone. I had just enough time to go back to Gram's, change clothes—since I smelled like Cliff's basement—and get to Lou's by noon.

# CHAPTER THIRTY-NINE

A BRAND-SPANKING-NEW LEXUS—dealer sticker still in the side window—was parked at the curb in front of Gram's. I parked behind the Victorian and went into the house through the kitchen.

Sitting at the head of the dining room table was Trip Kipling, my former boss, drinking coffee and eating a piece of Gram's coconut meringue pie.

Trip is sort of like local royalty, heir-apparent to the family fortune his father, known as Big George, inherited from his lumber baron forebears. Trip is actually George Kipling III. "Trip" for short.

My mother hovered over him with the coffee pot. "More coffee?" He nodded. She poured.

"More pie?" My grandmother held the pie plate, the last pie wedge—the piece I'd had my eye on—suspended on her fanciest pie server. At the ready, should the prince require more pie.

*Ugh.*

He gestured toward his plate with his fork. "No, no, thank you. This is delicious."

I stood a moment in the doorway, watching my mom and Gram simpering and fawning over him like two serfs whose cottage His Majesty had deigned to enter.

*Blecch.*

I cleared my throat. Gram turned, excited. "Look who stopped by!"

"Hey, Trip," I said. *Nice of you to stop by and scarf down my dessert.* Snarky was ticked.

My mother stood mute, staring like a starstruck teenybopper.

"Hey, Mom!" I said. She jumped. "Why aren't you at work?"

"I, um, decided to take a half day. Errands to run." She was probably meeting Duncan, if she could tear herself away from His Highness, that is.

Trip said, "Nice to see you, Mackenzie."

"You too." I said the polite thing instead of what I was thinking. *What the heck do you want, Trip? You fired me, remember? Not over that yet.*

Gram looked at my mother. "Let's leave these two to talk." Gram started out of the room. My mother stayed put, giving one last glance of longing toward Prince Trip. *Good grief, woman. Get a grip.*

Gram turned around and dragged my mother by the arm out of the dining room.

I sat at the table and used the pie server to eat the last piece of pie right out of the pie plate. A little thing like table manners will never come between me and Gram's coconut meringue pie.

I asked, between bites, "How did you know where to find me?" I was surprised Trip knew the whereabouts of a mere servant like me.

"Chief Bronson told me," Trip said.

I'd seen the retired police chief at the Veterans Day ceremony. "How did he know—" I stopped. Police know stuff. "Never mind. What brings you here?"

"First off, I want to apologize for the abrupt way things ended with us."

I'd worked for Trip as his administrative assistant. "Oh, you mean how you unceremoniously fired me with no warning?"

"You know that was on my father's orders. I didn't have a choice. He fired me that day too. Remember?" Trip had never been able to live up to his father's expectations. I'd felt a little sorry for Trip that day—definitely Kinder, Gentler Me's choice.

He went on. "I have a business idea I wanted to run by you."

I thought, *Gee, Trip, I don't know if I want to give up this great job I have going through Lou's junk.* I said, "I'm kinda busy these days."

He held up a hand. "Hear me out. Chief Bronson and I were golfing the other day and got to talking. He's retired, but he still wants to keep his hand in investigations. But he doesn't want to have his name associated with anything publicly. So, he asked me what I thought about opening an agency."

"What kind of agency?"

He paused, I assumed, for dramatic effect. "You ready for this?" He paused again. "I'm opening . . ."

*Another pause? Get on with it already!*

". . . a detective agency."

I choked on my pie. "Wait. What?"

"Yup. You heard me. A detective agency. Me and Bronson, but without any public connection with him. He's a high-profile personality in this area, you know."

*Ah, yes, Chief Bronson. Big fish in a small pond. Like Big George. Like you wanna be, Trip.* "Is there enough going on in Three Rivers to support a detective agency? We've got cops already."

"We figure on working the whole area, the surrounding communities, rural areas. Chief Bronson says there's a lot of stuff going on out there. And even Three Rivers has a seedy underbelly. You'd be surprised."

I knew about some of that stuff, of course. And I had personal experience with being attacked, having my apartment firebombed, and then being robbed. But did my sweet little hometown really *have* an "underbelly"? And if so, was it "seedy" enough for what we were talking about here? Trip and Chief Bronson thought so. What did I know?

"What's all this got to do with me?"

Trip cleared his throat. "Okay, well, I told the chief you used to work for me, and he knew that already, of course."

"Of course."

"Anyway, he said he was impressed with the story about you in the paper and your skills. And I know you're amazing at being organized and all that. I agreed with the chief that you are impressive, of course."

"Of course." *Impressive. Yup. That's me.* Impressive Badass smiled.

Trip took a deep breath. "Here's the idea. We open an office. I provide the money up front. Chief does the investigations. And you—"

"Stop right there!" I stood as I smacked both palms against the table. "I'm *not* interested in going back to being your 'Gal Friday,' as my grandmother says, or as my mother puts it, 'some man's flunky.' If that's what you want, you can just forget it!"

Badass was in the house. *Impressive as hell. Got the message, Your Highness?*

His eyes got wide. He held his hands up and sat back in his chair. "Whoa, whoa, whoa! No! Absolutely not! Not that at all."

I sat back down, slowed my breath, crossed my arms, looked him in the eyeballs. "Okay, what then?"

He smiled and leaned toward me, elbows on the table. "I was hoping you would help us get things set up, and then you could work the investigations side, too, with the chief. Learn the ropes. Get your investigator's license." Trip looked down at the table. His voice got quiet. "And maybe, down the road, I might even get into that side of things too."

My turn to sit back in my chair. I looked at him for a long moment. "You? A detective. A private investigator. Seriously?" Snarky wondered, *Ooh, what's Daddy gonna say about that?*

Trip shot me a defiant look. "I wanted to be a cop when I was young. Did you know that? My father had a royal fit. Said being a cop was beneath the family's *dignity*." Trip's hands flew, air-quoting left and right. "He said that, as a *Kipling*, I needed a *real* profession, like lawyer or doctor. Being a public servant was what *other* people do. And I knew what that greedy old snob meant by *other people*."

I knew what he meant too. I come from a long line of *other people*.

Trip pounded a fist on the table. "I swear to God, I'm just so sick of living under the old man's thumb! He said he's handed me everything my whole life, that I've accomplished nothing. Nothing!" He put his face in his hands for a moment, then looked up, his tone measured, defiant. "Well, it's time I do something for myself, something *I* want. And I'm going to *prove* to him I can do it!"

Powerful motivation in wanting to prove a critical parent wrong.

We sat in silence for a minute or two, while he drank the last of his coffee and I allowed the last hunk of meringue from the pie to dissolve on my tongue. I pushed the pie plate away as Trip let out a big breath and looked at me. "Well, what do you think?"

I shrugged. "What would I be exactly? Not a partner?"

"You'd work for the agency."

"An hourly employee?" He nodded. How would this be any different from when I worked for him at Kipling Financial? Didn't seem like I was gaining anything, except *maybe* something down the road. And my fate would be in his hands.

Badass whispered, *No way. You gotta grab fate by the short hairs.*

Anxious countered with, *Oh, but a bird in the hand—*

Badass scoffed, *Leaves you with a palmful of poop.*

I needed to control my own future. I had money in the bank—a lot by my standards—thanks to my late ex. I could make an investment, buy myself a life.

I said, "What if I *am* a partner? I could still get things up and running. But I don't want to sit around doing paperwork or taking messages. I'd want to be out of the office, in the field sooner rather than later."

I heard Snarky. *Ooh, 'in the field'? What is this? The FBI?* I ignored her. I felt a little rush thinking about all this.

Trip said, "I have more than enough money to get this going. I know you don't have—" He stopped, looked around the room. "I'm sure you're strapped right now." His look held his unspoken question: *If you're not strapped, why are you living with your grandmother?*

I got huffy. "Don't you worry about how strapped I might be. What kind of money are we talking about up front?"

Trip shook his head. "No, Mackenzie. No. You don't get it. I *have to* start this on my own. I *want* to do this. And I want you"—he cleared his throat— "*need* you to be part of it. How about coming on as an employee, and down the road, once we've gotten established, you can be a partner. We can make that official in a contract so you'll know what you can count on. But I'll cover all the expense for starting this up. No financial risk for you or Chief Bronson. What do you think?"

I leaned back, drumming the fingers of my right hand on the table as I contemplated the ceiling, considering. After several beats, I looked at Trip. "Okay, hypothetically, what would I be making as an employee?"

He grinned. "What would it take?"

I smiled. I'd heard of "the catbird seat," but never in a million years did I think I'd be the one sitting in it.

# CHAPTER FORTY

'VE USUALLY BEEN ON the desperate please-hire-me-I'll-take-anything end of conversations with potential employers. I never thought I'd hear, "What will it take for you to come work for me?"

But here was Trip asking exactly that, and here was me saying, "More than I made before."

Trip said, "Gosh, I thought you'd be so flattered you'd do it for nothing."

It took me a beat to realize he was joking. This was new. Trip never joked before. He was always stressed, dead serious, and until the day he fired me and cried, I never saw any display of emotion.

Now, here he was joking. Smiling, upbeat, hopeful, determined. New and improved, this was Trip 2.0. Maybe getting fired by his father was a good thing. Maybe now, free from the old man's shadow, he could be his real self. He might even be charming. Who knew.

I said, "Sorry, no, I don't come cheap." Not anymore.

"Um, what were you getting before? My father was the one paying you."

I told him. He looked shocked, as in, *Wow, I had no idea people worked for so little.* "Seriously? You were worth twice that," he said.

I smiled. Yup. Catbird seat. Me, in it, sittin' pretty. "So twice that, then."

He nodded. "We can do that."

*Dang. Should have asked for more.* I decided to go for it. "I'll need vacation pay, paid holidays . . ."

Trip nodded.

". . . and I want PTO too."

"What's that?" he asked, and I explained.

He looked shocked. "People have that? Getting paid for just taking a day off?" *Geez, what planet is this guy living on?*

"Yep. And I want medical insurance. Dental and optical too."

"Huh? Okay. *This* is why I need *you.* You *know* about all this stuff," he said.

Snarky was tempted to snark. *Stuff like what? What life is like in the real world of us* other *people, instead of life in the rarified environs of the privileged and well-to-do?*

Trip pleaded. "What do you say? Please?"

I pretended to be reluctant, while Rational Me was screaming, *Take the deal! You can have anything you want! Take. The. Deal!* If this were a game show, I was about to cash in.

I gave a huge sigh, just for effect. "Well, I need to think about it. Can I let you know after Thanksgiving?"

Trip 2.0 grinned. I'd have to get used to the grinning. We both stood. He grabbed my hand and pumped it. "This is great, Mackenzie. Sure, you take your time. Think about it. No problem."

I looked at the clock. I needed to get to Lou's—pronto. I led Trip to the front door.

At the door, he said, "One more thing. I don't want to call this agency anything remotely connected to the Kipling name or anything related to the chief's involvement." He handed me a business card. "I thought we'd use our names, Trip and Mack. What do you think?"

I looked down at the card.

## TRIMAK INVESTIGATIONS

*Holy Brangelina!* "I'm flattered."

Three interlocking circles formed the logo. The address was on River Street, not far from our former office in the old bank building. "We're not going to be renting from your father, are we?" Already, it was "we."

Trip beamed. Proud. "Heck no! I bought the building myself. I'm going to start moving into the new office, and I'll call you next week to nail down the details. Maybe open first of the year, if not sooner."

I waved the card at him. "You had all this in place before we talked. Pretty sure of yourself, weren't you?"

He grinned the kind of grin you'd expect from a rich kid who always got the puppy for Christmas or the new bike for his birthday. "I appreciate you, Mackenzie." He blushed, then looked me directly in the eye. "I *need* you." Sincere Trip. Another part of Trip 2.0 I'd have to get used to. "Let me know what you decide," he said and left.

I watched out the front window as he drove away in his Lexus.

Gram's landline rang. She answered and said, loud enough for me to hear, "Yes, Lou, she's just leaving!"

I hollered as I ran out the backdoor, "Tell her I'm sorry!" A Lexus might be in the future, but Lou's was in the present.

I drove up Grand, turning on River Street toward Lou's. I didn't have a Lexus. I didn't have a Jaguar. I had a used Ford full of crickets. But with money in the bank and a job with full benefits, soon I'd be rolling through town in some slick new wheels. And Badass Me was thrilled at the prospect of real investigation work down the road.

Isn't life interesting? We can feel hopeless at times, the future grim. But, as Gram says, "Just when you're ready to give up, something comes along." I'd been set back to square one by recent events, and now, something had come along. Things were looking up—way up.

I ignored Anxious Me as she whispered, *What goes up must come down.*

# CHAPTER FORTY-ONE

I GOT TO LOU'S AT a little after one on Monday afternoon. As we organized her collection of used books, I told her about Trip's offer.

"You really want to be involved with that bunch of crooks?"

I knew Lou had nothing good to say about Trip's father ever since Big George had tried to railroad his project through the downtown area. Lou and the other small business owners had fought it and won.

"It's got nothing to do with his father. It's just Trip," I said. I didn't mention Chief Bronson.

"Just watch your back, okay?"

I assured her I would and said I'd keep helping her until we got things squared away. She appreciated that.

I filled her in on Riker's confession. When I mentioned the bruise on his cheek, she became angry. "How can people do that to their kids?"

"Can't be sure it was his dad," I said.

"Oh, like maybe he *walked into a door?* Get real, girl." She was right. It was the kind of excuse battered partners use when covering for their abuser. "I slipped in the shower." "I tripped over the step." Riker hadn't made an excuse for the bruise, but I hadn't asked him either.

As we sorted through a box of vintage jewelry she'd scored at an estate sale, Lou said, "I know something about abuse."

I got quiet. She took a deep breath and went on. "I was nineteen. He was so sweet in the beginning. Gifts, flowers, compliments. Then after the wedding, he became a different man. Controlling and angry." Her husband cut her off from her family and friends, told her who she could see, where she could go. He demanded an accounting of every moment of her day. He controlled the finances and gave her only enough for groceries. She had to beg for extras "like new shoes. Extras!"

"I can't imagine you putting up with that," I said. Lou was so confident, had such sass.

"I was young. Eventually, I felt like I was nothing. Hopeless. Helpless. I just took it." She shook her head. "I'd never let anyone do that to me now. I'm older and a lot wiser."

"Did he ever hit you?"

"Trust me, if that jerk had ever laid a hand on me, he'd be dead. No, he never got physically abusive, but he was intimidating as hell. He was a big guy. All he had to do was stand there, and I'd start shaking."

"How awful," I said.

"I've thought a lot about those days. I think the verbal and emotional stuff is almost worse than the physical. You can't see it. There aren't any bruises, so nobody can tell."

"Did you ever say anything? To your family?" I could imagine what my big brother, Greg, would do if someone was abusing me.

"My family? My father wasn't much different from my husband. My mother put up with all kinds of nonsense from him her whole life. I think she was relieved when he died. The one time I tried to talk to her about my husband, she just changed the subject. I took that to mean, 'Suck it up, Buttercup.'"

I couldn't imagine not having support from my family. "I didn't know you were ever married, Lou. Gram never said anything."

"It's ancient history. He filed for divorce after we'd been married three years. Told me he couldn't stand to be with anyone as stupid and weak as I was. He found another victim, divorced me, and married her. I wish I'd warned her."

"You know where he is now?"

"In prison. Life." A shadow crossed her face. She looked at the floor. "He killed her."

"Oh, my God, Lou. I'm so sorry."

"Let's not talk about it anymore."

We got back to the task at hand: sorting and pricing the jewelry. I thought about Gram. She'd never tolerate abuse. Neither would my mother. I couldn't imagine any of my siblings in that situation. Sure, sad things happened. Cheating, divorce, death. But as far as I knew, nobody was dominating and controlling anyone else.

If they were, I'd be able to tell. Wouldn't I?

# CHAPTER FORTY-TWO

## Still Monday

M ONDAY AT FIVE, WE'D just sat down to crockpot chicken and rice. My mother sat across from me. Chloe came into the dining room and jumped on the empty chair beside my mom. Then she placed her front paws on the table, opened her mouth, and dropped something onto my mother's plate.

My mom screamed and jumped up, knocking her chair over. "Oh my God! What IS that?"

I stood and craned my neck to get a closer look. "Why, Mom, that there is a dead cricket. Chloe gave you a gift. I told you she didn't hate you!"

"Oh my God! That's disgusting!" She took her plate to the kitchen and scraped her dinner, cricket and all, into the garbage. "I'm leaving! Duncan's place doesn't have crickets—or cats!" she hollered and slammed out the back door.

Still on the dining room chair, Chloe looked at me with an innocent expression that said, "What? What'd I do?"

I frowned at her. "Chloe, that was not nice, and you know it." I swear she shrugged her shoulders at me before she hopped off the chair, and, tail high, sauntered off. *Little stinker*.

I decided we'd had enough of the crickets, so I called Webster's Auto after dinner. Dan himself answered and told me he was closing soon but would wait for me.

Cricket's crickets seemed to be multiplying by the minute as I drove to Webster's. They chirped wildly as the car moved, and at every stop sign, they fell silent.

When I explained what was going on, Dan said, "So your last car got torched, and now this one's got crickets?" He shook his head. "You don't have much luck with vehicles, do ya?"

"Oh, I have luck—it's just all bad. Can you get rid of the crickets?"

"No problem. Just leave 'er here overnight." He called to his runner, a young kid named Matt, who drove me back to Gram's.

# CHAPTER FORTY-THREE

## Tuesday, November 20

TUESDAY MORNING, DAN WEBSTER called to say I could pick Cricket up after noon. "Found another problem," Dan said. "The seat heater on the passenger side was messed up. Wouldn't shut off even when the car wasn't running. Thing like that will kill your battery pretty quick." He chuckled and added, "But probably kept your crickets cozy."

*Thanks a lot, Greg.*

Dan went on. "I'll disconnect the seats—don't want the fire hazard. I'll call you when she's ready to pick up."

I thanked Dan and assured him I'd gone this long without the luxury of toasty buns. I was pretty sure I could make it through another winter.

I had an errand to run, so Gram let me use the Buick—for the last time, I hoped. I backed out of the garage and headed down the alley.

I'd gotten a voicemail from Jillian an hour earlier. She asked me to meet her at the high school in Jason's classroom.

Room 110. She said, "I need your help with something I can't figure out. Maybe you can." She'd appealed to my ego. Or maybe it was Nosy who agreed to meet her.

I turned onto First Avenue. Gray clouds scudded across the sky ahead of a predicted cold front. I'd dressed in a heavy sweater of Gram's, in a Scandinavian pattern, blue with white knitted bands around the shoulders. Under the sweater, I wore layers from Stephanie. My feet, cozy in wooly socks, were laced up inside the new-to-me Doc Martens.

I'd watched the morning weather report with Gram and my mom over coffee. Our local weather people don't have fake names like big city weather folk. Nobody named Kurt Breeze or Stormie Day around here. The weather guy—sorry, meteorologist—on our one local channel goes by his actual name—Stuart Klump. I'd have definitely changed that.

That morning, Stuart told us, "The weather is changing in our neck of the woods today." Gram laughed when I suggested we have a drinking game for every time Stuart uses the phrase "our neck of the woods." Stuart is also fond of the phrases "garden variety showers" and describing light rain as "not a washout, by any means."

We'd laughed out loud one morning when he told us, "Take an umbrella today, but only if you're going outside." That one caused my mother to snort coffee out her nose.

Today, according to Stuart, morning temps in the low 40s would be dropping through the afternoon. Rain would turn to freezing drizzle later in the day.

As I turned onto Woodson Street toward the high school, a light mist settled on the windshield, and after several blocks, the mist turned icy, pelting the windshield with fat globs of snow. A few at first, then more, until I had to keep the windshield wipers going.

"Here it comes," I said aloud. Winter at last. We'd had that drought all summer. Then a torrent of rain at the beginning of the month. Now winter.

Icy roads. Piles of snow to clear from driveways and sidewalks. Old folks slipping on ice, breaking hips. Cars skidding into intersections. Freeways covered in massive pileups. Cars and trucks sliding into ditches.

*Snowstorms and semis and slide-ins! Oh my! Blizzards and ditches and ice! Oh my!*

"Oh my gosh! Stop!" I yelled. Anxious Me sounded like my mother, who was certain we'd all end up "dead in the ditch somewhere."

No danger of that happening at the moment since the snow melted as soon as it hit the pavement. And Gram's old boat of a Buick weighed a ton and could hold its own against a little sleet. Even so, I drove a little slower than I would have on a dry, clear day, tapping my brakes at stop signs.

As I neared the high school, I replayed Jillian's voicemail in my head. She'd found something—she couldn't tell exactly what. Jason was at home, she said, cleaning the house.

Thanksgiving week, there's no school for the kids in Three Rivers. The gun deer hunting season starts the weekend before Thanksgiving, and so many people pulled their high schoolers out of school for hunting that the school district eventually decided everyone should just take a break. I'd loved those extra days off when I was in school.

I'd taken a huge chance the day before. I'd assumed Jason was teaching, forgetting about the school break. Jason could easily have come home while I was in the house.

I pulled into the parking lot at Three Rivers High. I recognized Cliff's gray Taurus—now Jillian's.

The only other vehicle in the lot was a dark blue SUV. I assumed it belonged to a custodian cleaning while students were off, or maybe a teacher catching up on grading.

I dodged snowy plops as I trotted into the school. My Doc Martens squeaked on the wood floor, my footsteps echoing, bouncing off the lockers that lined the hall. Memories of high school wafted back, triggered by that unique school smell of floor wax and green soap.

I paused at the bottom of the three-story stairwell, smiling at the memory of kissing Billy on the steps as we passed between classes. We'd been late to classes more than once, making out in hidden corners of the school. We'd been voted Cutest Couple in our class, probably because we were the only couple who'd stayed together for all of senior year.

Jason's classroom was on the ground floor in the group of science classrooms near the gym and the swimming pool.

I got to room 110. The door was open. Jillian sat on the far side of the room, perched on a tall stool at one of the metal-topped tables and facing the door.

"Hey Jillian," I said as I walked past the tables and shelves of beakers, test tubes, and Bunsen burners. The room smelled like years of experiments. On one wall hung a poster explaining scientific investigation methods, and on another, the periodic table of elements. Another spelled out safety procedures in case of disaster. A first aid kit was attached to the wall above a sink beside the teacher's desk.

"Hey, Mackenzie, thanks for coming," she said with a smile.

As I got close, I noticed a scratch along her left jawline. It looked fresh, and a light bruise had started to form along it.

"Ouch. That looks like it hurt," I said.

Her hand went to her jaw. "It's nothing. I'm just clumsy," she said. She didn't offer more than that, and I didn't press.

Jillian wasn't in her usual schoolgirl getup. Today she wore jeans and a white sweater with a red cardinal made of sequins on the front. A long red scarf was draped around her neck.

"Pretty sweater," I said.

She smiled, looked down, and ran a hand gently across the cardinal. "Aunt Florence has such beautiful things. Loves birds. This is one of her favorite sweaters. It's such a waste that all her clothes are just hanging in her closet. Uncle Cliff doesn't let anyone touch them. Sometimes I sneak a sweater when he's not around."

I remembered the purple sweater with the little daisies she'd worn at the hospital. Anxious had a thought. *More than a little creepy that she's talking about Florence and Cliff as if they're still alive, don't you think?* Kinder, Gentler Me chalked it up to grief.

Jillian looked down, stroking her sleeve as she shook her head. "Mmm, mmm, mmm. Such a waste." She looked up and inclined her head toward me, lowering her voice. "Don't tell anyone, but sometimes I wear her robe. It's just so beautiful, so soft . . ." Her voice dropped away, a dreamy look on her face. Then she giggled and came back from wherever she'd gone. With a serious look, she whispered, "Don't tell anyone."

I shrugged. What did it matter? Florence and Cliff were gone. "Your secret's safe with me," I said. "You wanted to show me something?"

"This is Jason's classroom," she said, looking around. "He's like a genius. He runs the STEAM programs and the AP stuff. You know? Those classes for the brainy kids?"

"I've heard of that." I chuckled. "Wouldn't qualify myself."

She smiled back. "Me neither. Never was as smart as Jason. Never as good at anything." Her expression shifted. "He was born first, you know. We're twins, but it's like he took all the brains, and there wasn't anything left for me." She frowned and looked away. "He won the awards, never me. Never me." She'd gone to a dark place.

"I'm sure you had your moments," I said.

"Ha! With Jason around, nobody else *ever* has a moment! No way. It's all Jason, all the time. All. The. Time." Her eyes widened.

I didn't want us to continue down Sibling Rivalry Lane since, as a middle child, I'd spent plenty of time on that street. I shifted back to matters at hand. "So why did you want to meet me?"

She paused a beat, then shifted on the stool, reached down, and produced a small, clear glass jar from under the lab table. "Come over here and look at this."

I walked around to her side of the table to stand next to her. She opened the jar and raised it toward my face.

I leaned away. "What is it?"

"I'm not sure, but it smells familiar. I smelled it at the house, and then I looked in Jason's room while he was gone. I found the jar there in his bedside table." She wiggled the jar toward me. "Smell it."

I wrinkled my nose, shook my head. "No thanks."

"I thought maybe you, being as you're so smart, could help me figure out what it is."

I could almost feel my head swelling, but I took the modest route. "Nah. I wasn't that great in science class. I only passed chemistry because my brother Greg helped me."

"Well, my brother is a genius, so he was no help at all," Jillian said with a wry laugh. "He's so brilliant, he has no patience for my dumb questions."

"But he's been a teacher for years. He must have *some* patience."

"Yes, he has plenty of patience with these kids," she said, then frowned. "Just not with the people in his family."

"Ah yes, it can be like that." I pointed at the jar. "What do you think the stuff is?"

Jillian said, "I have no idea." She lowered her voice. "Jason's always experimenting with stuff. He experimented on our cat once, and it died." She paused, her face stony, looking past me. "It was my cat."

"That's awful," I said.

She smiled, coming back to the present. She held the jar toward me again. "C'mon. Help me figure this out." She smiled bigger. "Just smell this."

I should have remembered how it was on the playground. How the older kids tell some younger sap, "Smell this," and the little dope gets a faceful of something vile.

Yep, I'd fallen for it on the playground. And yep, I fell for it again in the chem lab. Like a trusting little dope, I leaned in.

In a flash, Jillian dumped the powder on the tabletop, took a handful of my hair, and shoved my face down into the stuff.

She body-slammed me, throwing her six-foot frame full-force on top of me as she held my face in the powder.

I tried to arch my back, but she pressed down harder. The edge of the metal table dug into my ribcage, my arms pinned under me.

Helpless. Powerless. Unable to move, I held my breath for as long as I could. Then I gasped in a snootful.

I felt the effects immediately—dizziness, then confusion. My eyesight blurred. My nose stung. I coughed and gagged. She held me down.

My thoughts jumbled, and my stomach lurched. Whatever this was, it was powerful stuff.

"That's right. Breathe in big. Then you fall down, go boom."

Through an increasing haze, disoriented, I remembered my mother saying that when I skinned my knee. "Aw, did you fall down, go boom?"

Jillian's voice became child-like, singsong. "Uncle Cliff fell down, boom, down, boom, down, boom." She grabbed a hunk of my hair and pressed my face down harder, her voice menacing, cold. "Now, we go up the stairs. Then you fall down, go boom."

A three-story drop over the railing from the top floor? Go boom, indeed.

Through waves of dizziness, my mind getting foggier by the second, I tried to piece things together. Jillian. Cliff. Fall. Boom. Dead.

I'd be next.

Through the fog, I sensed some part of me deciding *not today.*

I held my breath again, and then, with every ounce of strength I could muster, I straightened my back, wriggled my hands to the table's edge.

I pushed up as hard and fast as I could, head-butting backward—smack into Jillian's face.

She yowled and swore as her weight eased off me for a fraction of a second.

Adrenaline surging, I pushed back hard. She stumbled back against the stool and lost her footing, landing on the floor with a loud "Oof!"

Woozy and disoriented, I saw double one second, and then everything wavered and blurred the next.

My eyes watered, my nose ran, my throat burned. *What the hell was that stuff?*

I saw the door—two doors, actually—and hands in front of me, ran toward what I hoped was the real one. It was.

I staggered into the hall, swiping my hands across my eyes, wiping snot on my sleeve.

The walls and floor of the hall moved and shifted. Which way was out? Left? Right? Which way led to the parking lot and freedom?

I heard Jillian yell behind me, and I ran, stumbling forward to the right.

Wrong choice. Not the parking lot. This hallway dead-ended at the gym.

# CHAPTER FORTY-FOUR

THE GYM DOOR CREAKED loudly as I shoved it open. I ran, the soles of my boots squeaking against the gym's hardwood floor. I wiped my sweater sleeve across my nose and mouth. No use. With every breath, I sucked the whatever-it-was deeper into my system. Dizzier with every step, I stumbled into the locker room at the back of the gym.

The gym door squealed open behind me. Jillian hollered, "There's no way out!"

I was in the boys' locker room, and Jillian was correct. No exits except back into the gym. I looked around for anything I could use to defend myself. Hand weights? Nope. I'd have settled for a tennis shoe, but the locker room was clean. The custodial staff was top-notch at Three Rivers High.

I spotted an open locker and pulled my cell phone from my jeans pocket to call for help. I was trying to squeeze myself into the locker when Jillian grabbed me by the sweater and pulled me away. My cell flew across the floor.

I wrenched myself free of her grip. I ran toward what I thought was the door back out into the gym, but it opened to the showers instead.

Toilet stalls, urinals, and beyond those, the sinks, showers.

I looked up at the windows. Wire mesh covered the frosted glass. No escape.

I needed to wash my face, rinse my mouth, stop the burning. I beelined for the sinks, but Jillian was on me as I passed the urinals, which were mounted to the concrete wall at floor level.

She tackled me. I went down hard, my breath knocked out of me as I hit the concrete floor, my face level with a urinal.

She yanked me forward by the hair, shoved my face into the porcelain, and held me there.

I gasped for air and inhaled the chemical stench of the urinal cake. A wad of toilet paper and a soggy cigarette butt clogged the drain. The custodian had missed a spot.

Jillian held my face in the urinal and reached up to hit the flush button. *Floosh!* Water streamed against my nose. I clamped my mouth shut. This was not exactly how I had planned to get the nasty powder off my face, but it was working.

I arched my neck up enough to grab a breath before she shoved me down again.

*Floosh!* The water was helping me. She obviously didn't realize that. Another flush. Another breath. My head felt clearer.

Flush. Breath. Clearer still.

Mind clear. Anger rising. Adrenaline surging.

She didn't notice as I inched my right hand forward. I clawed my fingers around the wad of soggy toilet paper, the cigarette butt, and the urinal cake. I jerked to my right side, reached over my left shoulder, and smashed the wad into her face, smack on her bruised jaw and the side of her mouth.

"Aacckk!" She gagged and sputtered, letting go of my hair as she lifted partway off me. As hard as I could, I jabbed my left elbow into her side.

"Oof! Son of a—!" She swore and reared back.

I shoved myself up to all fours. She rolled off me.

I made it to my feet, wiping water and God-knows-what from my face. She scrambled to her feet and lunged at me.

I dodged and jammed my right fist, hard, up into her solar plexus.

She staggered back, bent over. I kicked and landed a Doc Marten to her chin, and she hit the floor.

I shook my head to clear the last of the fog. My cell was in the other room, on the floor by the lockers. I took a step toward it.

She scrambled forward and reached for my ankle. I stomped her wrist. She pulled back, came to her hands and knees.

I was on her, like stink on, well, urinal cake.

I gave her one more boot to the face and another to her gut. The air left her body, and she flattened to her stomach on the concrete. Still.

I knelt on the small of her back.

"Get . . . off . . . me," she said with a groan.

"Not a chance," Badass Me said, fully in charge. I reached for the long red scarf she'd wrapped around her neck and yanked back on it. Her head came up, and I used the scarf to tie her hands behind her.

Badass was proud. *Yep, trussed her up like a calf in a rodeo. Extra impressive badass move. Oh yeah!*

I pulled her to her feet, pushed her to the empty locker, and tried to cram her inside. Realized quickly that a six-foot female will not fit into a five-foot locker. Rational Me, while not a science genius like Jason, recognized simple geometry when it came into play.

I yanked her to a sitting position on the floor between the locker and the bench bolted to the floor. I tied the end of the scarf around one of the legs of the bench.

"That'll hold you," I told her. She moaned.

I picked up my cell phone, still okay despite careening across the concrete floor. My hands shook as I called 911, explained the situation. I slowed my breath as I sat at the far end of the bench to wait. I was afraid if I sat too close to Jillian, I might do her bodily harm. More than I'd already inflicted.

Her voice pleading, child-like again, Jillian said, "You're not very nice. That was really mean, shoving that nasty stuff in my face."

"Tell me about it," I said.

"You know it was all Jason, never me. He's mean. He's controlling. He hit me this morning, scratched my face. You saw it. I'm innocent. He did it all. Please let me go . . ." She went on and on, how Jason was the one who killed Cliff, how he'd used that stuff to disorient him, make him dizzy. "He even killed the canaries," she said.

That put me on alert. "What about canaries?" I'd seen them myself, of course, but I played innocent.

"Uncle Cliff got them just a month or so ago. But they were so noisy. Jason hated them, so he poisoned them. Stuck them in the basement."

Jillian went on to say all the things a person would say when trying to shift the blame from what they did to somebody else. I ignored it all until I couldn't stand to listen to another syllable.

"You know what? I don't see Jason here. You're the one who tried to kill me today, so I don't believe a word of your story.

I think you did it all. Killed the cat. Killed the canaries. Killed Cliff. You did all that. The cops are on the way, so save your breath."

"You're wrong. And stupid. Whatever!" she said, shooting me a dirty look and continuing to mutter not-very-nice things about me.

# CHAPTER FORTY-FIVE

MINUTES LATER, I HEARD someone call my name from the gym. "In here!" I hollered, and a second later, my mother and Gram burst into the locker room.

"What the—?" I expected cops, not these two. "How did you know I was here?"

Gram spoke. "Velma was driving by and saw the Buick in the parking lot. She called to ask what I was doing at the school, so I figured you were here. I called your mother at the bank, and here we are. I just had a feeling . . ."

Ah, bless Gram's intuition. And her nosy friend, Velma. "Well, I'm thrilled to see you!"

My mother hadn't said a word. Just stared at me. When she finally found her voice, all she said was, "What . . . how . . ." and then stopped, blinking back tears.

"Mom, I'd hug you, but I'm kind of a mess here."

Gram said, "You're okay, aren't you?"

I shrugged and pulled the soggy sweater away from my stomach. "I'm fine, but your sweater isn't."

"Pish tush. Don't worry about my sweater." She asked again, "Are you okay?"

I nodded and then pointed toward Jillian. Evidently, they hadn't noticed that I had a six-foot strawberry blonde tied up.

Gram spoke first. "Jillian? What's going on here?"

Jillian saw an opportunity and started spewing the biggest load of garbage in the whiniest voice I'd ever heard. How I'd lured her to the school, drugged her, tried to kill her by drowning her in a urinal, tried to cram her in a locker, and now had her tied to the bench. "Please, can you help me?" That last bit was delivered in the child voice she'd used earlier.

Gram looked at me, questioning. I shook my head, rolled my eyes. Gram believed me, of course. I carried the proof of what really happened. Drenched in urinal water, I probably had bruises blooming on my face and maybe even burn marks from whatever the hell that caustic powder was. I didn't need a mirror to know I was a mess.

Of course, Jillian had a size eight boot mark on the side of her face, and who knew where else. Half the red sequins that formed the cardinal on her sweater had been torn away in the struggle, and she looked more than a little soggy from when I'd introduced her face to the contents of that urinal. But I was sure I looked worse.

My mother suddenly regained her voice. She loomed over Jillian. "It's obvious what happened here. My daughter would never—*never*—act that way. Your whole story is, well, *bullcrap*! I ought to slap you silly!"

*Impressive. Go Mom!* My mother raised her right hand, but Gram grabbed her arm before she could make contact.

"I feel the same way, Barbara, but let's just wait for the police." They sat on the bench, Gram nearest me and my mom on the other side of Jillian, each holding on to the scarf that held her down.

"This is one of Florence's scarves, isn't it?" Gram asked.

Jillian, all sweetness and innocence, smiled at Gram. "Yes, it is. And this sweater was one of Aunt Florence's favorites."

"Cardinals are my favorite birds," Gram said.

Jillian went on and on about the sweaters, the robe, the closet. Gram listened patiently. My mother shot me a look from behind Jillian, swirling her index finger next to her temple. Every part of me agreed with my mom.

*Yep. Jillian be crazy. A few sequins short of a full bird.*

A few minutes later, the police arrived. Three officers I didn't recognize, followed by Officer Burns, who looked at me, recognition dawning. "You again? Prentice. Uh, Mackenzie, right? Seems every time I turn around, you're there."

I gave him the highlights of the afternoon as he jotted notes. His brows shot up at the mention of the powder. He sent an officer down the hall to seal Jason's classroom, keyed his shoulder mike, and requested a HAZMAT team come to the school.

I promised to go to the hospital to get checked out. Gram assured Officer Burns that she'd make sure I kept that promise. Meanwhile, the other officers untied, cuffed, and Mirandized Jillian before leading her to the locker room door.

I turned toward the door when I heard a man shout, "What's going on here?" Jason had arrived. He shot his sister a look, then got close to her face. She started to sob. I heard him hiss, "What did you do now, you stupid cow?"

Jillian blubbered. "She was asking—Sorry. I thought you—Sorry. I thought I could help."

Jason got in her face and said something I didn't catch. She cried harder. One of the officers suggested—strongly—that

Jason back away. He did. The cops left with Jillian. I heard her wailing all the way down the hall.

Jason came into the locker room. He looked at me. "You're a mess. What did that crazy sister of mine do to you?"

I gave him the abbreviated version. When I mentioned the mysterious powder, his eyebrows shot up. "What kind of powder?"

"I don't know. It made me dizzy, disoriented. Any idea what it was?"

He shrugged. "No idea. Did anyone from the school see you? Anyone at all?"

Odd question. "No, nobody. Just me and your sister here."

"Good. I don't want to be the topic of gossip. I have my reputation to protect."

"How did you know she was here?" I asked.

He paused. "The custodian noticed someone had been in my classroom and called me. I came right over and heard the noise down here. What else did she say?"

I told him how she tried to put the blame on him for Cliff's death.

He shook his head. "She's always been unstable. Should have had her committed. Did she say anything else?"

"Nothing. Just that the canaries were dead. She said you poisoned them."

"What canaries?"

"She said Cliff had canaries. You weren't aware of that?"

"Never saw any birds. She's more unbalanced than I thought, imagining things."

Now, that was interesting. How could he not be aware of the canaries? Wouldn't he have heard them singing?

Curiouser and curiouser.

Jason said, "The sooner we put all this behind us, the better. Get Jillian the help she needs, sell the house, and move on."

Gram spoke up. "Jason, your aunt Florence was a good friend of mine, and seeing your sister in that cardinal sweater reminded me of how much I've always admired her beautiful things. Do you suppose, since you want to sell and move on, that I could take a peek in her closet and maybe have one or two things to remember Florence by?"

He considered, then gave a shrug. "Okay, I guess. I'll be at home all day tomorrow clearing things out if you want to stop by."

Jason told us he'd follow his sister to the police station and left. My mother drove her car back to work, and I rode shotgun with Gram in the Buick.

Gram reached over to pat my leg. "You were very brave back there."

I didn't feel brave. Everything hurt. I felt the fight's strain in every muscle. My lips were getting puffier by the second, and my teeth felt like they'd been jarred out of place from being bashed against the urinal.

Gram said, "I'm proud of you. You've got sisu, girl. Sisukas!"

I tried to agree with Gram, but when I tried to say, "Yes, sisukas," it came out more "Yeth, thithukath."

She laughed, and I tried to as well, but it hurt too much. I ended up crying instead all the way to the ER.

# CHAPTER FORTY-SIX

### Wednesday, November 21

G RAM AND I RANG the bell at Cliff's a little after ten o'clock on Wednesday morning. Jason opened the door and gave us a blank look as if he had no idea who we were.

I, for sure, didn't look quite like myself, with a dark bruise on my cheek, a swollen upper lip, and a growing bruise around my right eye. No chipped teeth, for which I was grateful.

My ER visit the night before was quick. No sign of concussion. All vitals normal. Nothing needed stitching. Sent home with a "be sure to call if anything changes." But today, everything ached.

"Good morning, Jason," Gram said. "You said yesterday that we could come and look through Florence's things?"

He stared at us a moment and then gave his head a quick shake. "Of course. You caught me—never mind. Come in." He took a step back, and we stepped into the living room.

I'd seen it all before, but Gram gasped and said, "Oh dear. I had no idea!"

Jason said, "Yes. Quite a sight, isn't it?"

I wouldn't have thought it possible, but it seemed that the piles of boxes had doubled since I'd been in the living room the previous week. Piles upon piles upon piles. I couldn't say anything, of course. Couldn't say, "Oh, you've been rearranging." Couldn't give away the fact that I'd been poking around where I had no business poking.

On top of one stack were some of the birdhouse projects I'd spotted on the basement workbench. And the box labeled KOREA. No sign of the birdcage.

Anxious Me felt a tingle of panic. *Had Jillian been clearing things from the basement, covering up evidence? Did I need to call Heather? Hadn't heard a peep from her about the dead birds, the pipe, or the spots on the basement steps.*

Jillian was in police custody, so things were out of my hands. Not my business what the cops did or did not do from this point forward. And Jason was probably just clearing clutter, getting ready to sell the house. Rational Me voted for that.

I wanted to do more snooping since we were in the house by invitation now. Maybe I could come up with an excuse to get back down into the basement.

Jason leading the way, we came to the dining room. Gram saw Brett Favre and gave out another little, "Oh, dear."

"He's cardboard," I said quietly, steering her past the cutout.

"He's creepy," she whispered.

"He's cardboard," I whispered again.

"I mean him," she said, with a nod toward Jason as we wound our way forward.

"Also cardboard," I said. Gram tried to stifle a laugh. It came out as a snort.

"Is there a problem back there?" Jason said in that teacher-in-charge voice I'd heard before.

"No, sir!" I said. Gram giggled, and I shot her a warning look that clearly meant, "Stop goofing around, or we're gonna get detention."

We came to Cliff's room. The double bed had been rumpled before. Now, the bedding had been stripped away and lay folded neatly at the foot of the bed. Jason's penchant for neat and orderly was evident. A half-dozen big black trash bags were lined up next to a large stack of cardboard boxes, flattened for the recycling bin. The treasure trove of AS SEEN ON TV boxes I'd spotted before were stacked neatly under the windows in order by size.

Jason stepped into the closet, pulled the string overhead to turn on the light. He stepped out. "All of Florence's things are in there. This is the last space to clear in this room. Your timing is good."

I glanced around the room. I didn't see another closet. "I'm curious. Where did Cliff keep *his* clothes?"

"Usually just thrown on the floor or stuffed into that dresser." Jason gestured toward a four-drawer chest in the corner, its drawers partially open and empty. "He wasn't particular about his clothes." Jason rolled his eyes, adding, "Or anything else."

I assumed Cliff's clothes were in the black trash bags in the corner. "Are there things of Florence's we should set aside for your sister?" I asked.

"I don't know why Jillian wanted to wear this old lady stuff." He looked at Gram. "No offense."

"None taken," Gram said, but her tone told me otherwise.

Jason continued. "No sense saving anything for Jillian. She's going to be gone a long time."

I didn't expect Jason to be sentimental about a dead woman's clothes. But his lack of compassion toward his sister seemed harsh. But maybe he was just a black-and-white thinker. No room for foolish sentiment, just the facts. No gray area for Jason. All or nothing. Right or wrong. While part of me understood the appeal of that, Kinder, Gentler Me thought he was mighty cold.

Gram said, "I'll be glad to take some things to my friend Lou. She can sell them on consignment for you in her store. Lou's Vintage downtown? Do you know it?"

"I don't need the money. Just take it all out of here." He'd given us an order. We nodded in unison. "I'll leave you to it." With that, he left the room.

Certain Jason was out of earshot, Gram said under her breath, "And you're welcome." She looked at me, shaking her head in disgust. "How rude!"

"Rude cardboard," I said, and Gram snorted again.

We stepped into Florence's closet, and a wave of Chanel perfume hit us both. Gram gave a little "Oh" and reached for my arm.

"You okay, Gram?"

"I just felt a little faint." She swallowed hard and whispered, "It's her Chanel. As if she's here with us."

I don't believe in ghosts, but in scary movies, the spooky thing often makes its presence known with a sound or a smell. Florence's Chanel was overpowering in this closet. Her signature scent, Gram had said. The scent of the woman, now the scent of her death.

I heard the catch in Gram's voice and looked at her. "We can come back another time."

"No, I'm fine. Let's do this now and be done with it."

I gave Gram a hug, and we set about clearing things out. This was a smallish closet, as was the custom when the house was built. A three-foot-long bar on each side, running front to back, for hanging items with shelves above each bar. Against the back wall, a row of hooks for Florence's scarves and her robe. Everything was, I guessed, exactly as it had been when Florence was alive. And it was packed full.

Dresses, blouses, skirts, and slacks. A white fur jacket that looked like rabbit. Another black fur jacket. A long red coat. Lots of red. "Red was Florence's favorite color," Gram told me.

Along the floor were pairs of high-heeled shoes. Some were stilettos. That explained the red pair in Jillian's closet.

Gram picked up a pair of blue heels. "Florence was taller than Cliff, but she loved wearing high heels. I asked her once about being with a man who was shorter than she was, and you know what she said? 'As long as his head is next to mine on the pillow, I don't care where his feet are.' Cliff loved being seen with her, so proud of his tall, beautiful wife."

Dozens of sweaters, folded neatly, were stacked on the shelves, and visible in the folds were images of the birds Florence loved. Bluebirds, chickadees, cardinals, and hummingbirds adorned the sweaters.

"Wow, Gram. This is kind of a shrine to Florence, isn't it?"

Gram didn't hear me. She was busy oohing and aahing as she removed dresses from the closet. She commented on different pieces. "I remember this one. She looked so pretty in this." With another, "She wore this to the dance at the VFW. We had such fun that night."

I was getting a history lesson on life with Gram and friends. As much as I loved to hear the stories, this was going to take forever if she stopped to reminisce over every piece. After a few minutes, I said, "How about we pack all this up and take it back to your house? We can sort it there and take our time."

Gram agreed. "The less time I spend in here, the better." She shivered and said again, "It's like Florence is here."

We packed everything into black trash bags as quickly as we could. Half an hour later, the closet was empty except for Florence's silk robe hanging on a hook. Gram removed it, and as it moved, the smell of Chanel hit us both again.

"Feel this," Gram said, running her palm along the length of the robe.

I felt its smooth coolness, admiring the embroidered flowers along the shoulders. "It's beautiful," I said.

"I might just keep this for myself," Gram said.

I remembered. "Jillian said she wears that robe sometimes."

Gram made a face. "What a weird girl she is." She shook her head. "Maybe I'll just give it to Lou to sell." She folded the robe and added it to the other bagged treasures.

I stepped back into the closet. As I reached to pull the string on the overhead light, I caught a strong wave of Chanel, as if the scent had suddenly intensified in that moment. Anxious Me shivered. Rational Me reasoned that Florence's perfume had soaked into the plaster walls over the years and moving everything around and out of the closet had stirred up the residual fragrance. Rational Me couldn't be sure if that made any sense, but that's the theory she was going with.

Before I turned off the light, I scanned the empty closet and noticed a small wooden box, maybe six-by-ten inches, on the floor in the far corner, in shadow. Its color so nearly matched the hardwood of the closet floor, I'd almost missed it.

*If the smell of Chanel hadn't caused me to hesitate—*

Rational Me interrupted that train of thought. *No such thing as ghosts.* The rest of me wasn't so sure.

I brought the box out into the bedroom, looking to be sure Jason wasn't coming. I told Gram what had just happened.

"It's Florence!" Gram said, delighted. She watched as I opened the wooden box. Perfume wafted upward from a bundle of letters wrapped with a lavender ribbon, the top one postmarked in 1951.

Gram looked. "Oh my. I bet they're love letters from Korea. Florence wanted us to find them! I want to read them, and Nathan will love to hear them. He was there. This is his history too."

I said, "But love letters? Isn't that a little too intimate, Gram? Would you want someone reading yours?"

"Oh, pish tush. What will I care after I'm gone to heaven what someone might be doing with the stuff I left behind here on earth? I'm sure Florence feels the same way."

"Well, you know her, uh, *knew* her better than I do," I said.

Gram lifted the pack of letters out of the box. "What's this?" She held up a small notebook with a red rose on the front. It had been under the letters. She riffled through it. "I don't think this is Florence's handwriting, but it seems feminine to me. What do you think?"

I took the book and scanned a few pages. "Who is Renaldo?"

Gram thought a moment. "Florence's brother-in-law, I believe, married to her sister Jean. Yes, that's right. Jason and Jillian's father."

"Then this must be Jean's journal. When did she die?"

Gram did a quick calculation, guessed at the year. I checked the last pages of the journal. "This was written just before she died."

Just then, Jason called from the hallway. "You about done in there? I need to lock up and get to the jail."

"We're done," I called. We'd filled three large trash bags.

Gram set the packet of letters back into the little box. I

slipped the journal into the waistband of my jeans. I wanted a chance to read it. Florence must have had a reason to keep it hidden.

Jason came into the room, and Gram told him we'd found the letters. I cringed and telegraphed a message: *Ix-nay on the ournal-jay.* I hoped Gram was receiving.

"Letters? Where? Whose letters?"

Gram opened the box and held it toward Jason. "They're love letters between Cliff and Florence. May I take them home to read them to my husband? He and Cliff were in Korea at the same time. I'll get them back to you."

After a long moment, Jason shrugged. "Keep them. I've got no use for them." Then he asked, "Was there anything else?"

Before Gram could answer, I said, "Nope, nothing else." She kept mum.

"You didn't find a diary, did you? With a flower on the front?"

Gram looked at the floor. I shook my head. "Nope. No diary." I was glad I'd put it in my waistband in case Jason wanted to search through the bags. "Was it important?"

"My mother kept a daily diary. We found them after she died. All but the final one. I thought it was here somewhere, but I never found it."

Puzzle pieces fell into place. Florence had found her sister's last journal and kept it. Why? Maybe just sentimental reasons, but my Spidey-sense told me to keep quiet.

I said, "I guess we're done here, Gram. Let's let Jason get going," I said, picking up two of the trash bags. Gram took hold of the third. Jason didn't offer to help.

He led us to the front door, and when we were on the porch, he said, "Well, goodbye then," and shut the door.

As we hauled the bags to the car, Gram said, "He's a bit of an odd duck, don't you think?"

I nodded. "If it walks like a duck and quacks like a duck . . ."

Gram laughed and finished the line. "It must be a very odd duck!"

Odd, indeed.

Gram dropped me at Webster's so I could pick up my car.

Dan Webster assured me he'd taken care of my "little problem" and that I should drive home with the windows open to clear the residual fumes from the insecticide he used.

As I drove Cricket home to the Victorian, all was quiet. Parked behind Gram's, I turned off the engine and sat a moment, savoring the silence. Then I heard a chirp. Faint but definitely there. A pause and another chirp.

"Are you kidding me?" I said aloud.

"Chirrup," came the answer. Sounded like a lone cricket had evidently lived through Webster's bug bomb. I felt a kinship with a cricket who could make it through something like that. The little guy deserved respect.

I was done fighting. "Okay, Jimbo. You can stay," I said.

"Chirrup." Mutant Ninja Cricket was a survivor.

# CHAPTER FORTY-SEVEN

I SAT ON THE PINK comforter in the Rose Room Wednesday evening, reading Jean's journal. She felt vulnerable, she wrote. Afraid to go to sleep at night. Worried that she wouldn't wake up, that someone might hurt her. Worried that she might get up confused and hurt herself.

She'd gotten a lock for her bedroom door, partly to keep others out but also to keep herself in. A sliding bolt she installed above the doorknob. More than once, she awakened to the sound of the doorknob turning.

And one night, she heard a voice outside the door, a young child saying, "Mommy? Mommy, can I come in? Are you awake, Mommy?" Jean had ignored it, pretending to be asleep. "Was someone there? Probably not. I imagined it. Or it was just a dream."

I'd heard Jillian using that childish voice. "Fall down, go boom," she'd said. And her mother had fallen down the basement stairs. I felt a tightening in my gut at the thought. Could

235

Jillian have killed her own mother? The picture on her dresser seemed so sweet.

I read on. Jean wrote pages of worries that she was losing her mind. Forgetting things. Misplacing things. Jillian found the stove burner on with nothing cooking. Jason found her coffee cup in the refrigerator, the milk in the cupboard. The shower left running for the whole day. Finding lights on when she was certain she'd turned them off. Again and again and again.

She assumed it was dementia. Her grandmother and her mother had had it, so it was probably her fate as well.

She wrote about Jason, how she relied on him to keep things going. How she depended on Jillian too.

Gram told me that when Jean died, the assumption was that she'd gotten confused during the night, maybe thought she was opening the bathroom door but opened the door to the basement stairs instead, took one step into the darkness, and tumbled to her death.

Completely plausible.

Jason and Jillian had done a great job taking care of their mother. No one suspected a thing. No one except their aunt Florence. She'd told Gram there was something "just not right" with those two. She never said what that something was.

Florence also told Gram that she didn't buy the whole "Jean getting dementia" business. Every time the two sisters were together, Jean was her old self within a short time. Laughing, remembering, talking just like always, no sign of memory loss. Judgment intact.

Curled up in the big pink bed, I read the last page: "Going to talk with Jason and Jillian tonight after they get home from work. Need to know if I'm going crazy."

I took my phone and googled Jean's name, found her obituary online. The last entry in the journal was her last entry on earth. She died that night.

As the saying goes, "That's all she wrote." I felt a chill. Gram would say someone had just walked over my grave.

# CHAPTER FORTY-EIGHT

## Thursday, November 22

THANKSGIVING MORNING. CLIFF WAS dead. Nathan was sad. Gram said she felt sorry for Jason, "all alone in that house," and invited him to join us for Thanksgiving dinner. She thought maybe having Cliff's nephew with us might cheer Nathan up too.

Heather texted me that Jillian would be spending this holiday in the county jail. Good. Right where she belonged.

I peeled potatoes at the kitchen sink, thinking about Jillian. I'd misjudged her. Badly. How? Because I'd seen her the way I saw Gram—a loving family member who had taken on the huge task of helping a relative in need.

I cut the potatoes into quarters, rinsed them, and covered them with cold water in Gram's big stock pot with a little salt added. I set them on the stove to boil, listening to Gram's high, sweet voice singing a hymn while she set the dining room table.

"When peace like a river attendeth my way / When sorrows like sea billows roll . . ."

Gram had certainly had her share of sorrows.

She sang on. "Whatever my lot, Thou has taught me to say / It is well, it is well with my soul."

So resilient, my grandmother. And just for the moment, all did seem to be well. I hoped it might last, but you know. Life.

I went back to thinking about Jillian. I'd assumed the best. I should have assumed the worst, and I hoped I wouldn't make that mistake again. She'd poisoned Cliff and tried to blame it all on Jason. Had there been any indication when we saw her at the hospital the day Nathan had that weird episode?

Had Jillian given me any sign of what she was up to? I wracked my brain, sifting through our several encounters. What had I missed? She seemed to genuinely care about Cliff and his well-being.

But there are liars in the world, sociopaths who get a thrill from deceiving others. Lying just to see what they can get away with.

And then there are the rest of us, who believe that old saying about honesty being the best policy.

Anxious Me whispered, *At least that's what you believed in the past.* Anxious was right. Lately, I'd been fudging, little white-fibbing, and sometimes out and out bald-faced lying. How had I become this person? Did I really think it was okay to do the things I'd been doing lately?

Are there circumstances where the end does justify the means? Heather had to follow the rule of law. Did that apply to her and not to me? Had I lost my moral compass? Lost sight of true north? Drifted into a world where there was no longer a clear sense of right and wrong? The world no longer black and white but shades of gray?

*Ooh, pondering the nature of good and evil. Well, aren't we profound?* I ignored Snarky and focused on peeling the sweet potatoes as I pondered on.

Besides bending the truth at times, I had put myself in risky situations. Why? Last month, figuring out what happened to my ex for myself, but also for his parents. And for him too. And I was still trying to figure out what happened to Cliff for my grandmother. Since it was for Gram, did that justify any means—lying, stealing, snooping, breaking in—to get at the truth? Evidently, yes, in my mind.

I put the sweet potatoes in a pot of water, added salt, and set them on the stove to boil. What about this new business with Trip and Chief Bronson? Didn't it mean I'd be doing more fibbing, more bending of the truth? I could justify doing things for the sake of family. Would there be a line somewhere in the future that I would refuse to cross?

The back door opened, and Greg's wife, Sarah, came in. Their three kids came tumbling in after her. Sarah gave me a hug with a "Happy Thanksgiving!" Gram hugged Joey. At twelve, he was already as tall as she was.

My mom hugged ten-year-old Charlie, tousled his straw-berry blond hair, and said, "You're even taller than when I saw you last week!"

Charlie said, "I saw a video online that said that's what grandparents always say every time they see you."

My mom laughed. "Well, it's true! And now I'm going to say it every time I see you, just to bug you!"

Charlie made one of those faces that says, *I'm trying to look annoyed, but I secretly like the attention.* The same face I used to make in middle school when Vince called me Banana-Belly.

Seven-year-old Violet came to me and held out three cat toys. "These are for Chloe." They'd had a cat for a couple of weeks, until Greg realized that what he'd been treating as a stub-born sinus infection was an allergy to cat.

Greg came in last, maneuvering a huge scratching post into the kitchen. This was not your average scratching post. More of a carpeted cat jungle gym with several platforms and hidey holes. There was even a hammock on one side.

Greg sneezed and then sneezed again.

"Let me take that," I said.

"Gladly!" Greg said and sneezed once more.

I turned to Gram. "Okay if we put it in the front parlor for now?"

She nodded. We carried the cat contraption together to the front of the house and set it a few feet away from where Tweet and Chirp's cage hung.

Chloe sniffed around the lowest platform, decided it was okay, then mounted the next and the next. Finally, at the top, she lay down, eye-level with the birdcage.

When she realized that Tweet and Chirp were her neighbors, she sat up, eyes wide. The tip of her tail twitched back and forth, back and forth, and from her mouth came a rapid-fire "eh-eh-eh" of kitty-cat excitement. I figured she saw this as a launching pad from which she could maybe, finally, get those birds.

Violet said, "I have a feeling that's going to be her new favorite spot."

I said, "I have a feeling you're right, kiddo."

Violet called to her dad, who was keeping a safe distance. "It's okay if we leave it here. Chloe likes it!" He gave her a thumbs-up.

I hugged Violet. "You can come visit Chloe anytime."

Greg heard that and hollered, "No problem. As long as your mother brings you," and sneezed once more.

# CHAPTER FORTY-NINE

AT ONE O'CLOCK THAT afternoon, we gathered in the Victorian's dining room. Candles glowed around the flowered centerpiece, and the air was heavy with the aroma of baked turkey with sage stuffing.

I missed the old days when all my siblings were together. This year, Stephanie was spending Thanksgiving with Mason in Atlanta. Little sister Deanne was with her in-laws. Brother Robbie was at home in LA.

I looked at the rest of the family around the table. Gram and Nathan. Greg, Sarah, and the children. My mother and Duncan.

This was Duncan's first time with the family group, and he seemed to be fine. No nervous adolescent twitching. Just relaxed, confident adult male behavior. Engaged in conversation. Like he'd belonged with us for years. Probably would even eat broccoli.

Jason had accepted Gram's invitation reluctantly. Dressed

in black, as usual, he sat next to Duncan, who asked, "So Jason, what kind of work do you do?"

"I teach at the high school. Chemistry and biology."

"Interesting. I admire anyone who teaches these days. Kids aren't like they were when we were young," Duncan said.

My mother said, "That's for sure," and then giggled, patting Duncan's arm and making goo-goo eyes at him. I was never going to get used to this version of my mother.

Jason said, "Kids aren't any different now. You just have to know how to handle them." I'd heard Jason's "teacher in charge" voice a couple of times now. I was certain he had no trouble controlling his classroom.

Gram chimed in. "Jason is quite famous in our little city, Duncan. He's won awards and was written up in the newspaper when he was younger. Isn't that right, Jason?"

He nodded. "Yes." We all waited for more, but he looked down and used the side of his fork to cut a piece of turkey on his plate.

I said, "Seems like your name is on every other trophy and plaque in the high school trophy case."

He eyed me, then spoke. "Yes, I did a few things back then."

I switched gears. "Jillian mentioned you might want to move once you sell the house. Brazil maybe? She said you went there in college, right?"

You know how it is when you're just making conversation, but you have the feeling you just hit a hot button? A shift in body language. A change of expression, like a shadow passing over their face. Subtle, but definitely there, and enough to give me pause.

I shook off the feeling. *Probably just my imagination after what happened with Jillian.*

Jason turned to Gram and smiled. "Mrs. Powell, did you enjoy the letters?"

Nathan heard that and brightened. "We were in Korea together, you know, Cliff and I were. Those letters—gosh, so many memories. Good times."

Nathan talked about his war experience as if it was the best time of his life. Time passing does that. The bad fades away, and the good remains. Someday, maybe, I'd be able to remember Billy without any of the bad stuff. Accepting Heather's amends was a big step in that direction.

Nathan went on about Korea.

Joey asked him, "Did you ever kill anybody, Pop-pop?"

Nathan grinned. "Did I ever tell you about the possum that got into my tent one night?" We listened, enthralled, as Nathan told the tale. In delightful Nathan style, the story had humor and suspense, and—most importantly—a happy ending for everyone, including the possum. Violet clapped.

I glanced at Gram. Her face glowed, so happy to have Nathan back—at least for the moment.

When dinner was over and Gram had tucked Nathan in upstairs for a nap, she announced it was time for our annual family walk. The official Turkey Trot in Three Rivers is held the morning of Thanksgiving Day before the feasts. Our family has, for years, walked together *after* Thanksgiving dinner. We call it our "Tryptophan Trot," and it's a great way to wake yourself up after the stuffing—of not just the bird, but ourselves.

Sarah declined, saying she was still getting over her cold and that the kids had had enough excitement for the day.

Gram turned to Jason. "You're welcome to join us."

He thanked her for dinner and excused himself. "I've got to get back to clearing out the house."

The rest of the family—Gram, Greg, my mother, and Duncan—headed to Rawley Park to walk. I would have gone along, but after my time in the urinal, I just didn't want to make the effort. I offered to stay home with Nathan and clean the kitchen instead.

Drying the last of the pots and pans, I envisioned a long nap in the cozy warmth of the big pink bed in the Rose Room.

As I hung the dishtowel on the handle of a cupboard drawer, I heard rapping at Gram's back door. I opened it and smiled. "Hey, Jason. What's up?"

"I think I dropped my wallet in the dining room," he said.

"Okay, go look," I said as I went back to the sink. "I'm just finishing up here. Did you want some more pumpkin—?" I didn't finish the question.

Jason attacked me from behind, his left forearm against my throat, the point of a knife against my right cheek.

"What the hell are you doing?" I managed to choke the words out.

"You know, don't you? Jillian told you."

"Told me what?"

"I know that you know about Brazil. My crazy sister told you, didn't she? Tell me, or I'll slit your throat."

"Can't . . . breathe." I squeaked out the words. *What is he talking about? What about Brazil?*

"I knew she couldn't keep her mouth shut. What did she say?"

"About . . . what?"

"Don't play with me. She used the drug on you. Told you I used it on them."

"Them? You mean Cliff? No . . . police said he fell . . . hit his head . . ." Stalling for time, hoping the family would come back or Nathan might come downstairs. Then, hoping Nathan wouldn't come down. Jason might hurt him too.

"Don't pretend with me. The cops are idiots. I'm not." He pressed his arm harder against my neck.

"Sorry." I managed to choke the word out.

He continued. "I caught the old man snooping around my lab in the basement. He found the canaries down there. That experiment didn't work." Jason sounded like a mad scientist. "He was going to call the cops. I hit him with a pipe."

*Aha! I was right about the pipe.* The momentary satisfaction was eclipsed by the pain in my cheek. The knife must have punctured my skin. I felt a warm trickle down my face. I winced.

Jason relaxed his hold a tiny bit and went on. He was certainly in a chatty mood, no doubt because he planned to kill me. "He ran. Fast for an old guy. I chased him upstairs. Caught him before he got to the front door. Shoved him. He hit the bricks. Nobody suspected a thing until my idiot sister opened her big mouth."

"Why? He was old and sick . . . you'd get everything anyway . . ."

"Ha!" Jason scoffed. "He wasn't sick. I tested my formula on him. It's genius. Other drugs combined with ayahuasca. Found that in the jungle during my semester in Brazil. Amazing stuff down there, just waiting for someone like me to market it. I'm going to be rich! Famous!"

"Found . . . what?"

"Timothy Leary changed the world with LSD. He was right! Psychedelics are the new frontier. My formula will change the world!"

I'd heard something about psychedelics being used to help people with mental illness, but not what Jason was doing. "You'll . . . change the world?"

"Freakin' right, I will! Just need to find the right balance. Tested it on animals. Jillian's freakin' cat."

*Jillian's cat? Was that the dead thing I encountered at Cliff's?* I gagged as the memory of that stench came back.

I'd heard that criminals sometimes feel the need to confess all. I was evidently a safe confessor because Jason went on. "I needed to try it on more humans. The old man was on the way out anyway. Perfect test subject. But then you had to start snooping around. Jillian's going to be put away. Nobody's going to believe her. And now you're the only loose end. I've got the cash, and I'm disappearing."

He'd probably cleaned out his own and Cliff's bank accounts, probably all his sister's money, too, and planned to disappear into the jungle.

"Disappear? How will the . . . Nobel Committee . . . find you, genius?" Snarky felt brave.

"Shut the f— up!" He squeezed tighter. "Now tell me!"

*Geez, shut up? Talk? Make up your mind, genius!* Snarky wasn't brave enough to say that out loud.

Rational Me said, "Your . . . mother? Did you . . .?"

He tightened his arm around my neck as he talked faster. "My mother would have done anything for me. She needed my help. That's where it all started. She had delusions. I could have cured her. I'll cure schizophrenia. Autism. Bipolar. A cure for goddamn mental illness! Just needed a few more subjects to test on."

*Oh my God.* Poor Jean's diary had been a record of her delusions. Regardless, Jason had used the formula, whatever it was, on his own mother and on Cliff. The cat, the birds, and who knew who else.

Jason was a monster.

I needed more time. The family would be coming back soon, I hoped. I managed to choke out a word.

"Diary."

He stopped talking. "What did you say?"

"Your mother's . . . last diary . . ." Maybe he'd let me go so I could get it for him, give me an opportunity to fight back.

He tightened his grip, pressing on my windpipe. "Dammit! I knew it. That last diary. I looked everywhere. It was with those freakin' letters, wasn't it? Tell me!"

He let up a little on my neck but pressed the tip of the knife harder against my cheek. "That's right. I found it. In the closet." I wanted this bastard to know he wasn't the only genius in the room. I was pretty dang smart myself.

He swore. "Dammit! Where is it now? Tell me, you stupid cow!" Same name he called Jillian.

I wasn't about to give him the diary. It didn't really say anything incriminating about Jason, but he thought it did. That was my only leverage.

He squeezed his fingers into the sides of my neck hard. "Learned this move in martial arts. Cut off the blood to the brain. Lights out."

"Can't . . . talk . . ."

He eased the pressure on my throat. "Tell me!"

I sucked in a breath. "Your mother knew what you were doing," I lied. "She wrote all about it. She knew everything."

"My freakin' mother! The bitch!" *Geez. Nice way to talk about your mama.* "Where's that diary now? Tell me!" He pressed into my neck again.

"I gave it . . . to the cops."

"Bull! They'd have contacted me by now. Where is it?" He twisted my head to the right, and I felt his hot breath in my face as he hissed, "Where. Is. IT?" With each word, he pressed his fingers harder against my throat.

I felt light-headed, the blood flow to my brain slowing. I had to keep him talking, keep stalling for time. "You . . . genius . . ."

"Damn right, I am! I need that diary, and I need to shut you up."

"But Jillian . . . knows everything."

He ranted on about how crazy she was, how everybody knew that, and how she'd be going away for a long time. He didn't notice as I inched my hand forward toward the counter, toward the cast iron skillet I'd just dried.

Minimal movement. Inching closer.

*Keep talking, jerk.* Almost there . . . just another inch.

She came out of nowhere.

I heard a hiss and a low "mrrrow," and in a flash, Chloe leaped onto Jason, digging her claws into his arm. At the same moment, I grabbed the skillet with both hands and, adrenaline surging, swung it up and back, smacking it as hard as I could against his head.

He dropped the knife and released my neck, cussing what Gram would call "a blue streak."

He waved his cat-clad arm wildly. Chloe dug in. He grabbed her by the scruff of her neck, pulled her off his arm, and threw her toward the wall.

He lunged toward me again. I raised the skillet, ready to strike.

Chloe, evidently trained in the martial arts of the back alley, wasn't about to back down. Chloe sprang onto the kitchen table, then springboarded onto Jason. She dug her claws into the back of his neck.

He swore and thrashed, banging into the table. Lost his balance and fell onto his back on the floor.

Chloe sprang free, then came at him again, landing hard on what I assumed was his favorite body part. He yowled, grabbed at his crotch, and, groaning, rolled onto his stomach.

Chloe scrambled out from under him in time to avoid being crushed.

Skillet in hand and following Chloe's example, I jumped onto his back and brought the cast iron down on his head with a clang.

He went still. I used the dishtowel I'd hung on the drawer handle to tie his hands behind him.

Badass was impressed. *Trussed him up, just like his sister! Yee-haw!*

# CHAPTER FIFTY

I WAS SITTING ON JASON, frying pan poised to smack him again, with Chloe standing guard at my side, when the family came back from their walk.

Greg, first one through the door, yelled, "Holy crap!" and ran to me. He took over holding Jason down. Duncan helped.

I scooted away on my butt, leaning my back against the lower cupboards, trying to calm my heart as my mother dialed 911. I hugged Chloe to my chest, letting her purring calm my frantic shaking.

Once Gram was sure I was okay, she went up to check on Nathan. I was grateful he hadn't heard the ruckus and come down. And I was relieved Sarah had taken the kids home after dinner, so they didn't have to witness the aftermath of the violence.

I was still shaking hard, but as we waited for the police, I managed to blurt out the details of what happened.

Jason came to and tried to get up, but Greg and Duncan let him know it was in his best interest to hold still. And shut up. Outnumbered, he complied.

Three officers and two EMTs arrived—nobody I recognized—and things happened in a blur. Jason was handcuffed and on his feet with an officer on each side, heading toward Gram's back door. He twisted to face us and yelled, "That f—in' cat is a menace! It should be put down!"

Gram crossed the kitchen lightning-fast, planted her five-foot-four self in front of his six-foot-four hulk, and jabbed her finger into his chest, emphasizing every word and saying, "You. Don't. EVER talk like that in MY house, young man!"

He glared at her. She glared back. After a moment, he broke eye contact, mumbled something that sounded like, "Sorry, Mrs. Powell," and looked down at his feet.

Evidently, the rule of "Gram says do, you do" applies beyond our immediate family.

As Jason was escorted from the house, Chloe, on my lap, gave a low growl in his direction, which I translated, *Don't even think about touching my human again.* I stroked her fur.

My mother patted Chloe's back gingerly. "Good kitty. Good kitty," she repeated.

Miracles do happen.

EMTs checked me over. I declined their offer to take me to the hospital. I just needed a little disinfecting and a butterfly bandage over the puncture on my cheek.

I gave my statement to the remaining officer and said I'd come to the police station and sign a formal complaint the next day.

My mother brought me a glass of water and offered to add a shot of brandy.

"Yes, please." I sipped it. Warm. Calming.

I don't remember who tucked me into the pink bed, but Chloe and I slept. She may have chased mice in her sleep, but mine was deep and, thankfully, dreamless.

# CHAPTER FIFTY-ONE

Saturday, November 24

'D SPENT FRIDAY IN bed, recovering. Vince called. He'd heard what happened from my brother Greg. I thanked him for his concern, assured him I was fine. He asked if I still wanted to go out sometime.

Nosy Me couldn't resist asking about his ex. "What about Lori? Are you two getting back together?" Nosy sounded like a middle-schooler. *Do you like her like her? Me or her? Check the box.*

He paused. "No way. We had a drink for old times' sake."

Before I could stop her, Anxious blurted, "Anything *else* for old times' sake?" *Geez, shut up! None of your beeswax what they did or didn't do!*

He cleared his throat, ignoring the question, his voice taking on that official investigator tone I'd found so attractive before. Now it sounded cold. "Hey, do you want to go out with me or not?"

I hesitated. A little too long.

He cleared his throat. "Huh. I guess that's a no. Take care," he said and disconnected.

Snarky jumped in. *Well done, genius. Alone again. Naturally.* She knows a lot of old songs.

Friday evening, Tansy and Jade stopped by to cheer me up with a giant package of red Twizzlers and a bottle of Chloe chardonnay. "In her honor," Tansy said.

We sat on the bed in the Rose Room, drinking wine and eating Twizzlers, bashing all the men who ever let us down. Chloe made herself at home in Jade's lap, curled up in her ankle-length skirt.

Jade and I raised our glasses, joining Tansy in a toast. "Men may come and go, but we three"—she glanced down at Chloe—"make that we four—will *always* have each other!" We clinked our glasses. Jade said, "Amen!" Chloe purred agreement.

Saturday morning, Heather stopped by as Gram, my mother, and I sat in the dining room. Heather had listened in as the twins were questioned. Each blamed the other, calling names and yelling like two children. "A whole lot of 'I did not!' and 'You did so!' Ridiculous! Nobel Prize? Matching tattoos? What's the deal with those two?" she said.

"Yeah, something just not right there," I said.

According to Heather, Jillian knew that Jason drugged their mother. "When Jillian confronted him, he insisted he was trying to help their mom. But he told her to keep quiet or he'd put something in her Cap'n Crunch. She kept silent. She claims he's dominated and manipulated her their whole lives. Said she attacked you to protect him, thought he'd be grateful. Makes no sense at all. She just snapped, I guess."

A judge had issued a search warrant for Cliff's house. Heather was sure they'd find what the DA needed. I didn't envy the officers who'd be digging through that hoard. "As long as they're at the house, there's a cat there who could use some help." Heather said she'd pass that along. I gave Heather Jean's journal, though it didn't prove anything.

I walked Heather to Gram's front door. She looked at my face—puffy lip, bandaged cheek, purply green eye. "You look like hell. Sure you're okay?"

"No permanent damage."

"You know, if you hadn't gotten all hot about that feather in his nose, we'd never have found out what really happened. And I heard about your new gig with Trip Kipling. Too bad. You'd be a great cop."

I touched a hand to my cheek. "No thanks. Don't need any more excitement."

She went on. "Being a cop isn't like being out there on your own. We've got training, equipment, and backup. And most of the job is writing tickets, handling rowdy drunks. Tame stuff ninety percent of the time."

"But that other ten percent?"

She smiled. "Okay, yeah, that can get your heart pumping." She looked wistful, as if she loved that heart-pumping stuff best. Part of me loved that, too, but I wanted to be free to take it or leave it on my own terms.

A couple of hours later, as we finished lunch (hot turkey sandwiches and leftover mashed potatoes slathered in gravy— the ultimate in comfort food), Gram got a call from Cliff's attorney, Max Rankin.

Since Max was also Gram's attorney and they'd been friends for years, she asked, and he told her that Cliff willed the house and all his "treasures" to Florence's cousin Sadie from New Jersey. The twins would not be benefitting after all, thank goodness. I hoped Sadie would sell the house to the Crandalls.

Max told Gram that Sadie would be arranging a memorial service in Three Rivers in the near future.

"That's wonderful," Gram said, wiping away a tear.

Max went on. To Nathan, Cliff left his Packers collection and Korean War memorabilia. Nathan clapped like a little kid at the news. Gram would be getting Cliff's collection of depression glass and all his vinyl records.

After she hung up, Gram said, "Sweet of Cliff to give us the records. We all used to go dancing at the Moose Lodge. Florence was a beautiful dancer. But what do we want with all that old glass and all the Packers stuff? Does that include that Brett Favre thing?" She gave a little shiver. "I just read that book about Swedish death cleaning. I don't need more stuff."

Lunch finished, my mother dished out the remaining pumpkin pie, refilled our coffee cups, and sat down.

I took a deep breath and said, "I have an announcement." Gram and my mother looked at me. Nathan was busy with his pie.

I cleared my throat. "I've decided I'm going to work with Trip and Chief Bronson, learn the ropes, maybe become an investigator."

My mother exchanged a look with Gram, then smiled and said, "That's nice, Mackenzie."

*What? No dire warnings about danger from my anxious mother? No predictions of horrible failure?*

Gram reached over and patted my hand, just like she did with Nathan. "Good for you, Sweetie."

Seriously? "That's nice" and "good for you"? In the past few weeks, they'd been bugging me about my plans. "What are you going to do now?" "You deserve better than a part-time job at Lou's." "How about going back to school? Moving to the city? Stephanie could help you . . ."

So much fuss about my future. And now, when I'd finally decided, this was the reaction? "Meh"?

But what did it matter? I was thirty-five. It was time to take charge of my life, create a future for myself. And this future had enough potential—enough challenge, enough excitement, and, I had to admit, enough potential danger—to keep all the parts of me happy. *Oh yeah.*

Later that night, thinking about my future with Trip and the chief, I sat in bed with my new Dell laptop. (Yes, I splurged on a new computer in anticipation of the big fat paychecks I'd soon be collecting.)

I played with some possibilities for my future TRIMAK business cards, trying on different titles for my future self. I typed:

MACKENZIE PRENTICE, DETECTIVE. *Nope, too pretentious.*

MACK PRENTICE, ACCIDENTAL DETECTIVE. *True, but nobody will get it.*

MACK PRENTICE, IMPRESSIVE BADASS. *No, too braggy.*

M. PRENTICE, PRIVATE INVESTIGATOR. *Definitely not. Too* Magnum, P.I.

*Get real,* said Snarky. *You're more Miss Marple than Magnum.*

*Be honest,* Rational Me said. Thinking about the female mystery solvers I'd watched on TV, read about in books, I typed:

MACKENZIE PRENTICE, AMATEUR SLEUTH

I looked at the screen. Autocorrect decided I meant to say:

MACKENZIE PRENTICE, AMATEUR SLUT

Snarky laughed so hard, she almost wet her pants.

COMING SOON: Book three in the series

# PAINTED LADY

A Mackenzie Prentice Mystery

M ACKENZIE PRENTICE DIDN'T EXPECT to find a dead body that morning. And she sure didn't expect it to be painted like that. In PAINTED LADY, Mack's artist friend Jade Kelly needs help. Jade's under suspicion, and her father's missing. Mack can't resist helping a friend in need and soon finds herself swept into the seedy underbelly of artistic counterculture and onto a living canvas of danger and intrigue.

Mack is thirty-five, has a touch of OCD, is addicted to sugar, may occasionally drink too much, and has those voices in her head, commenting on her choices. But she loves a good puzzle and admits she's nosy. In this third book of the Mackenzie Prentice Mysteries series, Mack's got a nifty new job and a bright future—if she's around long enough to enjoy it.

# ACKNOWLEDGMENTS

READER, THANK YOU FIRST AND FOREMOST for inviting Mack into your world.

Thank you, Michelle Rayburn (missionandmedia.com), for cheerleading, editing, designing, and consulting. You make it look so easy, and you make Mack look so good!

Thanks to Joe Coughlin for his patience and insight into police matters. (Any mistakes in that area are strictly my own!)

Thanks to eagle-eyed sister Carol Persons, first reader and editor, for your warm encouragement. (I'm not really sorry that you "got caught up in the story and forgot to edit." That's a good sign, I think.)

Thanks to daughter Katy Stevens for inspiring me and to daughter Lizz Berry for adding sprinkles of humor and fun to the first drafts; to both of you, thanks for help with marketing and all things online. The rest of the clan: Alex, Jenny, Laura, Dan, partners, and offspring—so grateful to have you all. And special thanks to the grandkids who inspired the characters—you know who you are.

To Laura, Paula, Mary Lee, Jane, Fern, Jessie, Liz, Ashley, Deirdre, and the other early readers—I'm so grateful you saw what I hoped you'd see in Mack's world. Thanks for your encouragement and for spreading the word.

Finally, as always, thank you, my darling Terry, for almost forty years of love and support. "Go for it," you said, so I did.

# ABOUT THE AUTHOR

MARY PIERCE IS THE AUTHOR OF three books of humorous inspiration published by Zondervan/Harper Collins: *When Did I Stop Being Barbie and Become Mrs. Potato Head*; *Confessions of a Prayer Wimp*; and *When Did My Life Become a Game of Twister*.

Mary spent the better part of twenty years writing for publication—books, articles, and a humor column for a national magazine—and as a speaker/humorist, traveling around the country bringing laughter and encouragement to audiences at women's wellness events and retreats.

She left the speaking circuit to care for her aging mother, who had dementia. After six years as a primary family caregiver, Mary returned to school, earning a Master of Science degree in Clinical Mental Health Counseling at the age of sixty. As a counselor/psychotherapist, she works with adults in transition who are dealing with depression, anxiety, and life changes. She specializes in trauma reprocessing and caregiver support, as well as grief support.

In the other half of her time, she writes—the Mackenzie Prentice mystery series and other projects. She also enjoys messing around with collage and assemblage as a mixed-media artist. (What is it about fingers full of paint and glue that brings such joy?)

She and her husband, Terry, share six children and eleven grandchildren. They make their home in Eau Claire, Wisconsin, a goldendoodle named after their favorite pizza place. Visit Mary at marypierceauthor.com.